CONTENTS

GW00382472

ADVENTURES
IN
AVALON

An Offbeat & Quirky
Adult Bedtime Story

by

GINGER MARIN

Illustrations by Jeanine Henning

Contact:
contact@bijouentertainment.com

ISBN 9780692737521

Book Design by Bijou Entertainment
Cover Design & Illustrations by Jeanine Henning

This book is a work of fiction. Names, characters, places and incidents are the product of the author's vivid and strange imagination.

Dedication

To those teachers who encouraged good thought; to those friends who encouraged good actions; to those creative people whose collective works and deeds sparked and nourished my imagination and helped open my eyes to a world filled with wonder and absurdity amid the chaos; to J Bartell whose support through the years has instilled in me the insight into becoming a better person all around.

PART 1

DISPATCH FROM AVALON

Reporter Discovers Lost Civilization of Cartoon People in Middle America

AVALON — In the County of Ligature-Upon-Avon.

Avalon is one of those quaint little communities that is somewhat lost in American space, neither here nor there but definitely somewhere.

The Avalon Defense Department, which most other places call a police department, lies just on the outskirts of town. I know because I've been there. Not by choice.

There's a lovely Town Center with small shops and surrounding single family homes, all nicely painted in pastels and jewel tones. It's kind of like visiting a tropical island without the island. The shops have those cute swinging signs attached just above the doorways that sway gently in the breeze when there is one, which is often or not at all.

Numerous family farms dot the countryside. Why, there's even a lovely river that runs through it.

Despite its small town feel, Avalon, oddly, has a high rate of speeders with hit and runs and numerous other strange crimes. The weather is also very strange as it changes abruptly. One minute it's raining cats and dogs and the next it's as sunshiny as a sunshine day can be.

It has four seasons as most American towns do, but with such strange weather, no one has yet to figure out what season it is.

The County strives to be more than it is and that's why in the past few years, it's been developing a bit of a cosmopolitan flavor with the addition of little ethnic neighborhoods, the biggest of which is 'The French Quarter', where most everyone tries to be French. There's even a 'Red Light District' for the town's naughty adults and, from what I've witnessed in the short time I've been here, there appear to be quite a few.

I stumbled upon the town recently while driving through Middle America on my way to Upper America and became as lost as Avalon. It was here that I experienced my first ever summertime hailstorm of such intensity in such a short span of time that it scared the bejeezus out of me.

And after having been horribly bopped by one of those hideous hailstones, I bumbled my way to the Avalon Defense Department for respite, expecting them to defend me from such goings on as this strange bump-inflicting weather. It was like walking into a 1940s police station, not that I've ever been in one, but I've certainly seen enough of them in the movies.

It was dark and small and crammed with desks and file cabinets everywhere. A big coffee machine was on a counter in a corner next to the donuts and there was nonstop racket from scores of clickety clacketing typewriters and the ringing big black telephones.

My fuzzy vision finally cleared sufficiently following the dastardly bashing I got from the hailstone and I could hardly believe what I was seeing. There were cartoon people rushing about doing their jobs.

At first I thought I might have entered the 'Twilight Zone' but everybody thinks that so I quickly dismissed the idea. Aliens? It was, of course, a very real possibility because aliens always land in Middle America, so I kept it under wraps and just sought out the most helpful cartoon person I could find or at least the most un-busy one. I figured if aliens went through all the trouble of building a Defense Department, a.k.a. police department, they would expect the occasional average person to stop by and seek their help.

I was really hoping to find a cartoon version of John McClane from the movie 'Die Hard' because he was so resourceful ... or even Popeye Doyle from 'The French Connection', since he already sounds like a cartoon ... maybe Sam Spade but he was what they call a P. I. or Private Investigator, so that doesn't count, but instead, all I could find was some little round dude named Officer WingWing who sat spinning in his chair and sucking on a lollipop. Oh well, I thought, perhaps he'd be able to point me in the right direction to get to Upper America.

Alas, this poor little bumpkin of a lad, who was dressed in his police blues with a large gold star and name badge pinned to his shirt and wearing short pants, of all things, was as clueless as I. He told me he wasn't allowed to talk to strangers and with that he got up and rushed out but not before falling flat on his face near the water cooler.

I had a feeling there was more to this place than met the eye so I went back outside, making sure the coast was clear as far as the weather was concerned, and found my way back to the town center where earlier I had spotted a newspaper office. Maybe someone there could give me the low-down on goings on around here.

The little shop-office was empty of people, cartoon or otherwise, but there on a door, serving as a tabletop in the center of the room, was a story ready for printing, 'AVALON DEFENSE DEPARTMENT SOLVES PENIS AND NUT CASE'. I could tell from my vast experience as an intrepid ace reporter that this case would have been a helluva head scratcher so I was eager to learn how they cracked it. I read on.

PART 2

The Case of the Missing Member

or

How John Sir Gwaine Bobolini Lost One of His Family's Jewels and How He Recovered It ... Well Sort Of

IT BEGINS at an old country farmhouse as heavy rain pours down and trees are lashed viciously by the nasty wind.

A police car is parked near the front of the quaint little house as the moon, peeking through storm clouds, is reflected in its windshield. Then just as the nasty rain comes to an abrupt halt, an owl hoots loudly, "Hoo-Hoo, Hoo-Hoo".

The inside of the farmhouse is painted all white and yellow with small daisies along the wallpaper trim. Then just then, a telephone rings.

General Schnitzkof, an old fart of 65, could be 68, answers the old-fashioned wall-mounted phone. Schnitzkof's one of those retired British Army generals and now the lead investigator of the Avalon Defense Department; you know the type, stiff upper lip, gruff and by the book.

"Schnitzkof here. Yes, yes, I'm at the scene now. Of course I am, Sir. You just called me here, remember? Where else would I be? We've found it! Yes, Sir. In the field, yes. Disgusting! Absolutely

General Schnitzkof and Officer WingWing
Avalon's Top Investigators

horrible. Shriveled like a date. My word, I'm beside myself! I beg your pardon, Sir? No, there is only one of me. So, how could I be beside myself? Well, I guess I couldn't be beside myself if I weren't two people. You're quite right. No, I didn't mean to confuse you. It's just an expression. I won't use it again. Getting back to the case now ... I don't know if the victim will survive. They've taken him to hospital, yes. I've given this top priority, being a man myself."

WingWing ... you remember him ... the little round rookie weirdo cop from the station house ... well, he runs in panting heavily. He's the General's trusted assistant. You'll soon come to see, even if you didn't already, that he's quite childlike yet occasionally astute. That's quite a combination.

"General, General Schnitzkof ... I am here oh, General of mine!"

"WingWing, can't you see I'm on the telephone?"

"Sorry, Sir, but ..."

"Shut up and wait your turn."

"Yes, Sir, but ..."

General Schnitzkof turns back to his phone conversation, "Hello, hello are you there?"

WingWing stands stiffly in the kitchen like a little wooden soldier boy, "I haven't moved Sir."

"Not you, you idiot.", barks Schnitzkof.

"Oh." WingWing now begins to innocently hum "Dum, dee, dum, dee dum, doodle dum."

Flustered, Schnitzkof tries to make up for WingWing's rude interruption, "No, no I didn't mean you, Sir, I meant the other idiot. Ah, ah ... what I mean to say is ... oh goodness gracious never mind. We're investigating to the top of our abilities. Good-bye, Sir."

And with that, the General clicks his heels like Adolf Hitler at a Nazi hootenanny and bangs down the telephone receiver.

"Now, what the hell do you want, WingWing?"

WingWing holds up a plastic baggy containing a shriveled somewhat elongated object. "I bagged it like you told me to. What do you want me to do with it?"

"Oh, my word, get that thing away from me. Go dangle it over the sink or something. Put it on ice."

"You want I should put it in the freezer?"

"No, it'll get freezer burn and someone might mistake it for a wiener."

"But", WingWing protests, "... it IS a wiener."

General Schnitzkof is momentarily taken aback, "Humm, so it is ... so it is."

The door suddenly bursts open and in strides Doctor Guido Guisseppe, the town's mustached, old-worldly wise, Italian accented county coroner with a flair for the rhythmic. He looks like he should be flipping a pizza or something. Perhaps even downing a glass of mediocre Chianti with a plate of fava beans. "Out of the way, coming through, Dr. Guido Guisseppe knows what to do."

Dr. Guido Guisseppe, County Coroner
Autopsy, Anyone?

WingWing, who's still standing in the center of the kitchen holding the baggy, chuckles like the little innocent that he is, "You made a rhyme!"

"Who is this moronic moron in uniform?", snarls Dr. Guisseppe.

"Wingwing, my assistant, and I'll thank you not to call him a moronic moron. I can do that myself!"

"Have it your own way, General Schnitzkof. But we're wasting time. That wiener must be taken care of before it's no good to anyone."

"Does anyone else want it?", asks Wing-Wing who then grabs a pot off the stove and drops the baggy into it.

"Only its owner, that Bobolini fellow", responds Dr. Guisseppe who now turns to the General, "They're looking after him quite nicely at the hospital and you know I think the chap's going to pull through. Amazing considering the loss of blood, not to mention the loss of virility. Where's the wife?"

"In custody.", replies General Schnitzkof.

Dr. Guisseppe spots WingWing holding the pot. "Holy cannoli, get that wiener out of the pot."

"Well I don't want to keep holding it."

With an odd twinkle in his eye, Dr. Guisseppe reaches his hand out, "Give it here. I'll take good care of it."

Hmmm ... sounds like there's more to this than meets the eye.

WingWing slowly extends the pot and Dr. Guisseppe gingerly removes the baggy. "A wiener in the hand is worth more than two in the bush, eh Wingwing?"

"I wouldn't know Dr. Guisseppe."

"Never mind about that now", barks General Schnitzkof, "I have an investigation to conduct. Wingwing, come along."

"Yes, General."

Schnitzkof quickly exits the farmhouse with WingWing in tow, "Dr. Guisseppe, we'll meet you at your office, later."

The door slams shut and Dr. Guisseppe is left alone in the kitchen admiring his baggy prize. He lets out an appreciative whistle.

Meanwhile, the General and WingWing are on their way back to the Avalon Defense Department, posthaste! WingWing turns on the radio, flipping around for a station he likes when he hears an advertisement for 'Wienerschnitzel'. He and the General exchange amused looks and WingWing bops to the beat.

They eventually arrive at the station and the General swerves his car to an abrupt halt in his special parking spot reserved just for him at the front of the seemingly large but actually small, quaint building. You can tell the spot belongs to him because of the large laminated photo of him nailed to a pole.

WingWing tumbles out of the car and, as he is wont to do when excited, trips and falls, this time into a rather deep mud puddle. Schnitzkof notices, but, like the gentleman he is, says nothing, although he does have a sympathetic look on his face. He's actually quite used to little WingWing's mishaps which are a daily occurrence. WingWing just gets up and brushes himself off as if nothing happened, as he too is used to his own failings. He then follows the General inside.

They find the lights dimmed with just two tired police officers, Mulligan and Stewball, typing up reports. They're like cartoon versions of Stan Laurel and Oliver Hardy. Stewball nods in the direction of the interrogation room. So, Schnitzkof whips off his coat and straightens his tie with a tug in a well mannered tradition before entering the darkish room, as WingWing follows wiping off his mud-splattered glasses.

Inside the interrogation room, Mrs. Bobolini, a Swedish flaxen haired beauty, who looks quite disheveled at the moment, is seated at a table running her hands over one miserably torn stocking. Schnitzkof inspects the damage as WingWing observes from nearby.

Then before anyone can utter a sound, the General pounds the table with his fist. BAM! "Okay, Mrs. Bobolini, this isn't going to be pretty. Admit it. You did the deed. You hacked it off like so much dead meat. As if it were some tumorous growth. Something to be expunged, obliterated. You revolting woman, you. Admit it, before I'm forced to smack it out of you."

WingWing winces, "Ouch!"

Mrs. Bobolini screams in her sexy Swedish accent, "I do admit it. I admitted it hours ago and I'll admit it again if you insist. I did the deed. I chopped it off like so much dead meat. As if it were a tumorous growth and something to be expunged and obliterated. And, I am not revolting!"

WingWing takes great delight in her admission of guilt "Ah, ha! She admits it. What do you want to do with her now, oh General? Shall we throw her in with the druggies and weirdos, the lesbians and prostitutes, the bad people ... all of them? Shall we put her in the cell, lock the door and throw away the key? Huh? Huh?"

"No, no, no, we can't do that just yet. She hasn't been formally charged. You should know that by now, WingWing. Haven't you learned anything?"

"Ah ... that crime doesn't pay, except sometimes. That the poor always get screwed because they can't afford a highfalutin lawyer. That it pays to be rich and thin and ... a stitch in time saves nine."

"Right you are, WingWing."

Schnitzkof then turns his attention back to the pretty Swedish criminal. "Okay, let's get down to it, Mrs. Bobolini. Brass tacks. The bottom line. Facts are facts. And the fact of the matter is we know you admitted to slicing the not quite so lengthy figure in question. But! ... and this is the real question now ... we want to know what you did to the left nut."

Mrs. Bobolini is aghast and her mouth twists opens like Edvard Munch's 'The Scream' before she's able to spit out, "Left nut, left nut? I did nothing to the nuts. What are accusing me of now? I don't know what's with the nut ..."

"What IS with the nut, oh General?", asks a bewildered WingWing.

The General tries another tact. He casually sits at the table with Mrs. Bobolini, taking his time, drawing circles with his finger against the wood grain. "Surely you know, Mrs. Bobolini, that your husband has been accusing you of tampering with the nut as well. He is in indescribable pain ... a phantom pain in the nut that is connected to the loss of the top banana, so to speak."

"I have no idea what you're talking about. Can you describe the pain?"

"I just said it was indescribable, didn't I? What do you take me for, Mrs. Bobolini, a fool? A moron? Well, that would be WingWing ... you know very well what I'm talking about."

WingWing howls, "He's talking about the phantom. The phantom pain."

For some strange reason what could only be called 'Phantom Music' begins to play inside the interrogation room and Schnitzkof, who is obviously oblivious to it, now paces about just as a wild windy draft flies through, displacing papers on the table and unnerving WingWing who shivers in fright and whispers, "The ... the .... phantom. It's here."

"I'm warning you, Mrs. Bobolini", Schnitzkof warns, "you tell me about the nut or ..."

Now, of all things, that Phantom Music gets louder and louder, just like you might hear in a movie or even on a TV show or in the theater, as the General continues "Or .... or ...

Mrs. Bobolini has had enough. Now SHE pounds her fist on the table. BAM, "Or what?", she screams and her pretty nose twitches uncontrollably.

And for some even stranger reason, the Phantom Music is now in a very real holding pattern, like an airplane circling the airport but without the airplane or airport, a staccato I guess you'd call it ... it's still holding strong. This is, after all, a community of cartoon people so of course the music is going to be that way. It's holding ... holding ... until ...

WingWing blurts out, "It'll be the rack for you, you ... you ... horrible man hating, vicious, butchering female fiend."

"How dare YOU?", screams Mrs. Bobolini, "You little moron; you little squirt from Munchkinland; you slimy noodle from hell; you little piece of ..."

Now Schnitzkof has had enough. "ENOUGH!", he shouts.

"Enough? Wasn't it enough that I've already been attacked once tonight? That I've suffered repeatedly at the hands of my lousy, stinking, rotten, wife-beating, beer-drinking, cartoon-watching husband?"

Apparently even cartoon people watch cartoons.

WingWing ponders for the quickest of moments, "Ah ... I don't think so."

"Shut up, Wingwing. I believe her. She is innocent of the nut. But not the other thing. She's already admitted to that. Now, it's up to the jury to decide if Mrs. Bobolini will get jail or lethal injection."

"What about the electric chair?", asks WingWing.

"It's not an option here."

"Too bad.", the little squirt comments.

And with that, the General and WingWing leave the pretty criminal, who's maybe a victim, Mrs. Bobolini, alone in the interrogation room.

Mulligan and Stewball are just staring in their direction as they exit.

"So did you hear all that?", demands Schnitzkof.

They both nod "yes" like puppets.

"Good! Hope you learned how it's done!"

The General then strides over to the coffee machine and pours himself a stiff one while offering WingWing his usual cup of warm milk.

The next day the sun rises over Avalon, bright and cheery as it does on many a mild sunshiny morning, before the weather decides to dance to a different tune.

Outside the Avalon Courthouse, people are milling about, waiting for the latest 'Trial of the Century' to begin. Two sets of protestors wave signs 'Free Mrs. Bobolini' and 'Cook the Bitch'.

General Schnitzkof and WingWing hustle through the crowd and enter the packed courtroom just as we hear a gavel banging loudly ... three times! The spectators and the jurors are whispering loudly because they are all very excited about the *latest* 'Trial of the Century'. The General and WingWing take their seats in the first row of the spectators' gallery.

Madame Judge
Crazy As She is Ugly

Madame Judge is seated on the bench. This 55 year old woman, could be 60, has a face the shape of a triangle and her dark hair is in an old-fashioned flip, held back by a white headband. It makes her look like a traditional and ugly as dog-butt Catholic nun. The black robe doesn't help.

She bangs the gavel one more time. "Order, order. I'll have order in my court or I'll have you all thrown out. This isn't a carnival. It isn't Nuremberg. So let's have a little order."

Well, of course, the mumbling continues for a bit longer, just so she can scream, "I said QUIET! ... Okay. The court in the county of Ligature-upon-Avon versus Mrs. Isabella El Marriacchi Bobolini who is accused of somewhat neutering, not to mention obliterating, a certain object belonging to her husband John Sir Gwaine Bobolini is now in session. How plea you?"

The Defense Attorney, whose oily hair is slicked back and whose mouth is filled with ratlike teeth, rises most regally, as if his oily hair and rotten ratlike teeth don't smell, "Innocent, Madame Judge."

Then, the equally snooty Prosecutor, who is really rather plain looking with the exception of his unusual comb-over consisting of precisely twelve strands of hair, each glued to his head with a dot of Elmer's, jumps up waving WingWing's wiener baggy. "Innocent, innocent? This is a farce. I have the object right here."

There's a giant "GASP" from the spectators and jury.

Madame Judge pounds her gavel yet again, "Mr. Attorney, call your first witness."

WingWing can't take his eyes off the wiener as he whispers to Schnitzkof, "Eeek! It looks even smaller than when I found it."

"That's because the air conditioning is on."

"Oh ... But I thought they were going to re-attach it."

The Defense Attorney rises, "I call Mister Bobolini."

"Can't do that my boy," reports Schnitzkof, "it's evidence. And you know what they say about evidence."

"No, what do they say about evidence?"

"Never you mind, WingWing, now be quiet. I want to hear what that Bobolini fellow has to say in his own defense."

"Is HE on trial?"

"He beat her didn't he? He deserves to be on trial, that weasel."

"What about the wiener and the nut?"

"SCREW THEM!", screams Schnitzkof which prompts everyone in the courtroom to react in horror.

"Well, I'd rather not.", says WingWing.

Mr. Bobolini, who looks an awful lot like famed record producer Phil Specter, who had his own 'Trial of the Century' a while back in Upper America - you may recall - walks gingerly and a little stooped over to the witness stand. His hair looks like he's wearing Specter's famous fright wig and he's got a thick black mustache which twists oddly on his crooked Italian face as he takes his oath to tell the truth, the whole truth and nothing but the truth. He then takes a seat on the witness stand while holding a white handkerchief to mop his sweaty Neanderthal-like brow.

"Mr. Bobolini", says the Defense Attorney, "you're under oath. So, tell us truthfully, did you ever beat your wife or do anything otherwise that might give the little missus a reason to wish you harm?"

In his very high pitched thick Italian accent Mr. Bobolini answers as truthfully as this sick prick can, "Never. I could never harm my beautiful, lovely, ravishing and gorgeous Isabella. I love her so much. My heart bleeds at the very thought of her."

"I think he means his wiener.", adds WingWing , under his breath.

"Shhh!", scolds the General.

"You mean you never held a gun to her head and demanded sex?", asks the Defense Attorney.

"Absolutely not true.", an indignant Mr. Bobolini sputters.

"You never held a knife to her throat and demanded sex?"

"Absolutely not true."

"You never held an ice pick to her ear and demanded sex?"

"Absolutely not true."

You never held a razor blade to her wrist and demanded sex?"

"Absolutely not true."

But you DO admit to having what you called "rough sex"?

"That is absolutely true!"

Well, the spectators react to the Attorney's ploy with a hearty "Ah HA!" They know the truth when they hear it.

"My Isabella loved to have rough sex. The rougher the better. We both loved it. We played together. Is it not the prerogative of a husband and wife to play? To enjoy? To experiment?" Mr. Bobolini now becomes increasingly excited. "To ... to bind ... to beat ... to punch ... to humiliate .... to rip out the finger and toenails ... to strip of all human dignity ..." ... and now breathing heavily, he screams "RIDE 'EM COWBOY!"

And just like in the interrogation room when we heard that strange Phantom Music, we now hear the whinny of a horse loud and clear, just as Mr. Bobolini comes ... out of his euphoria. "Oh, my goodness, that is so good. All in the name of matrimonial obligation?"

Good Lord, the man's a lunatic! Huge GASPS come from the shocked jury and spectators.

General Schnitzkof leans into WingWing, "I knew it, the dastardly devil. The weasel. He deserved it. Just hope the jury sees it that way."

"Gee, and I was just thinking that maybe I should get married."

"Quiet."

Mrs. Bobolini, who is seated at the Defense table, is in anguish; she sobs miserably and rivers of blackest black mascara stream down her pretty face. "You see what that lousy bum has done to me.", she screams.

Madame Judge bangs her gavel because that's all a judge can do at this point. "No more outbursts. You may leave the stand Mr. Bobolini. And take that rolled up sock with you."

The Prosecutor rises, "With your permission, Madame Judge, I would like to have Exhibit A released. Mr. Bobolini is due in surgery this afternoon."

"What is Exhibit A?", asks the Judge.

The Defense Attorney pops up, "The wiener, Madame Judge."

"Does the Defense Attorney have any objections to the release of Exhibit A, better known as the wiener?" she then asks.

"None, Madame Judge."

The jurors all crane their necks to see Exhibit A which is on the Prosecutor's table.

"On second thought", says the Prosecutor, sly devil that he is, "I think the jury deserves a better look at the exhibit so they know the full extent of this horrible vicious man-hating deed. With your permission, Madame Judge, I would like to have the wiener passed through the jury box. Please instruct the jury to look .... but only a quickie."

"All right, you may pass the wiener."

The jurors react as the wiener is passed along with their various "Oohs and ahs" and sounds of disgust ..."Yeechs, ughs, yucks, oh my gosh, eeewww", and whatever other words signifying revulsion that you can imagine. Then a juror actually faints, yes faints, and crashes to the floor which causes everyone else in the courtroom to become highly agitated.

"Enough. Remove the wiener.", demands the Judge, "It's obviously too much for some people to take."

"I thought it was too little.", WingWing whispers to Schnitzkof.

"Will you shut up, WingWing, and listen and learn something about how the law operates."

"I'm trying, my General, but this wiener thing has got my head all turned around."

The Prosecutor gets up, "Madame Judge, may I remind the court that there's still this business about the nut".

"The Nut? The Nut? No one said anything about a nut. If there's a nut in this case, then let's crack it!"

The entire courtroom of men react to the Judge's remark with their "Ooooohhhhhhhs, ughhhhhhhhs, aeeeks". Some are even crossing their legs. Cry babies!

The Prosecutor continues, "The phantom pain in the left nut."

Suddenly, there's that strange Phantom Music again. It's pretty low but it's there. Can you hear it?

A mysterious wild draft, just like in the interrogation room, wafts through the courtroom, causing the lawyers to grab hold of their paperwork before it flies wildly off the tables.

WingWing becomes increasingly frightened. "It's that Phantom again, General, it's baaaack." General Schnitzkof pats little WingWing's hand which calms him down.

"Mrs. Bobolini is also accused of tampering with the left nut.", says the Prosecutor.

Madame Judge then demands of the criminal, Mrs. Bobolini, who may indeed be a victim, "How do you plea with regard to the nut?"

"My client", reports the Defense Attorney, "is innocent of all nut charges, Madame Judge."

Madame Judge acknowledges exasperatingly, "That's what I thought. Mr. Prosecutor, what evidence do you have regarding the nut? I mean if it's a ..."

"NO, Madame Judge, don't say it!", a frightened WingWing blurts out.

The Judge ignores WingWing, just as so many other people do and continues on ... "phantom ...."

The wild draft swirls about the room causing havoc. The Judge's hair flips upward so she looks like 'The Flying Nun'. The draft is so strong, in fact, that WingWing is lifted right out of his chair. Schnitzkof quickly grabs his hand and reigns him in. Others in the courtroom react nervously.

"No evidence, Madame Judge.", says the Prosecutor, sadly, "The doctors cannot account for the strange lack of sensation related to the dastardly disappearance of the top banana, so to speak."

"I see. The jury will disregard anything they've heard related to the left nut. I am shocked that Mr. Prosecutor would try to sway the jury with such tactics as ..."

WingWing braces himself. Lawyers reach for their papers.

" ... phan ....", ha ha, ha, Madame Judge catches herself. She wags her finger at the Prosecutor in warning.

"I'm sorry, Madame Judge, I will try to do better."

"See that you do. Now call the next witness."

I will now call Officer WingWing to the stand. Madame Judge, this is the little ... ah ... officer ... who found the wiener in the field that dark and almost rainy night.", announces the Prosecutor.

"I see."

Hearing his name called, WingWing pops out of his seat and pads feverishly to the witness stand so fast that papers fly off the Defense Attorney's and Prosecutor's tables after him. The lawyers throw up their hands in annoyance.

Then, there's a loud thud as WingWing trips on a step and smashes his face into the side of the witness box. He rises, a bit unsteady, face flattened like a pancake, but not the least bit embarrassed, although he should be. "Ow! I hit my head. May I please be excused?"

"No, you may not.", shouts Madame Judge, "Be seated and shut up."

WingWing remains standing but quickly raises his hand to swear his oath.

"Do you Officer WingWing swear to tell the whole truth so help you God?", asks the Judge.

WingWing just stares at her with that stupid yet innocent childlike look on his face which has now unflattened itself.

"I said ... do you Officer WingWing swear to tell the whole truth so help you God?"

Still nothing from WingWing which causes the Judge to ask "What's the matter with the little round guy, is he deaf or something?"

The Defense Attorney offers this little gem, "If it please the court, you told the little gentleman to shut up."

"Listen you", Madame Judge scolds WingWing, "don't play games with me. Speak up when you're spoken to or I'll have you held in contempt. Is that clear?"

"May I speak now?"

"Oh, good grief. Speak, already."

"I'm ready, oh Judge. I shall speak the truth as I know it. I promise."

"Thank goodness. Now let's get on with it, shall we?", she says.

WingWing excitedly plops into the large witness seat, feet dangling like a small child's.

"Sidebar, your honor.", the Defense Attorney calls out.

"You may approach."

Both lawyers move to the bench and the Defense Attorney announces "Madame Judge, I'm not sure this ... ah ... fellow is competent to take the stand."

"Of course, he's competent.", protests the Prosecutor, "He's a police officer."

Madame Judge and the lawyers glance over to WingWing who's making strange noises into the microphone mounted in front of him. After a moment, the Judge says, "Looks like you'll both have to take your chances. Step back now and proceed."

Of course the lawyers do as they're told because that's what lawyers do even if they don't like it, especially that ratlike Defense Attorney. He's irked to say the least.

Then the Prosecutor says in his official prosecutorial voice, "Officer WingWing, tell us in your own words exactly how you found the wiener?"

"Well, it was rather soft and kind of small.", reports WingWing.

"No, no, no", admonishes the Prosecutor. "I don't want to know how you found the wiener. I want to know HOW you found the wiener."

"Oh. Well, I walked very carefully and slowly around the outside of the house, like I was told. I searched and searched, but there was nothing there. I then proceeded to search on foot in a diagonal path away from the house to the outhouse. There was nothing there. I then proceeded to search on foot in a diagonal path away from the outhouse to the barn. There was nothing there. I then proceeded to search on foot in a diagonal ..."

"Just a minute", says the Prosecutor, "Can you please speed this up?"

WingWing pauses, and then in exactly the same tone, continues "I then proceeded to search on foot in a diagonal path away from the barn to the road. There was nothing there. I then proceeded ..."

Annoyed, Madame Judge butts in "Hold on, you", she says to WingWing. "the Prosecutor just asked you to speed things up. Do you want to be held in contempt or what?"

"No, Madame Judge, I'm trying to tell you how I found the wiener. It was a long walk to the field where I eventually found the wiener but he wanted to know EXACTLY how I found the wiener. So it's a long story."

"Well, we don't want to hear any more of the long story", Madame Judge says angrily. She takes control of the questioning, "Let's wrap this thing up shall we? You found the wiener in the field, right?

"Right. But I didn't wrap it up. At least not right away."

"Was there anyone in the field who saw you when you found the wiener?"

"Just some cows. They were ignoring the wiener even though it was under foot."

"What were the cows doing?" asks Madame Judge.

"Eating grass."

"What about gas?"

"I'm sorry my Judge, I didn't mean to do a poo-poo."

"Not you, the cows. Did the cows do poo-poo?"

"I don't think I noticed."

Cows Like to Eat Grass and Daisies
Not Wieners!

"How could you not notice something like that? What kind of police officer are you? Didn't you keep any notes?"

"Yes, I made notes."

"Well, check your note book."

WingWing pulls out his note book from a little purse that he wears around his neck. "Let's see here. Dog doo-doo. Ah ... bird doo-doo. People doo-doo. Lots of cow doo-doo. No, nothing here about poo-poo."

"No poo-poo? I'm absolutely incredulous."

The Prosecutor stands, "Madame Judge, I must protest this line of questioning. What do cows and gas have to do with the case?"

"They're depleting the ozone layer. Isn't that reason enough? I can't believe I'm the only one in this court who cares about the ozone layer."

"I care.", says WingWing.

Madame Judge ignores Wing-Wing and tells the Prosecutor, "Finish your questioning of the little guy before it's his bedtime."

"Yes, Madame Judge. Officer WingWing, what did you know about the wiener and when did you know it?"

"Ah ... when General Schnitzkof told me about it?"

"Good. And what did you do with the wiener after you found it?"

"I measured it to determine if it was the wiener in question."

"And was it?"

"Was it what?"

"The wiener in question?"

"What's the question?"

The Prosecutor is now rightfully exasperated and damn well pissed off. His voice rockets off the courtroom rafters. "Was the wiener you found in the field on that dark and almost rainy night, the wiener belonging to the victim John Sir Gwaine Bobolini?"

Poor WingWing becomes terrified by the Prosecutor's loud obnoxious tone. He sputters, "I ... I ... I ... put it in a baggy."

"Geez, geez, geez! All right. Do you see the wiener anywhere in this court?"

"It looks like my baggy over there." WingWing points to the baggy on the Prosecutor's table.

"If it please the court, let the records show that Officer WingWing has identified the wiener inside the baggy marked as Exhibit A.", says the satisfied but rather exhausted Prosecutor.

"So be it. Are you through with this witness?", asks the Judge.

"I am, Madame Judge, thank God."

"The witness may step down but is advised not to leave town. I have some more questions about those cows that I would like answered at a later date."

"Thank you, Madame Judge. I am at your service." WingWing leaves the witness box and promptly falls flat on his face ... again. The Judge flags the Bailiff to get him the hell off the stand and WingWing's plopped back in his seat next to Schnitzkof. He whispers, "Well, my General, did I do good?"

"You were splendid, my little dumpling boy. A real credit to the force."

"Oh thank you, my General. I am so happy I did you proud."

Madame Judge demands, "Call the next witness."

The Prosecutor now calls Mrs. Bobolini to the stand. Her high-heeled shoes click across the floor and everyone reacts to seeing a very sexy and well put together criminal make her way to the witness chair. She's obviously wiped off all that blackest black mascara that had streamed down her face when she was wailing like a victim earlier.

Madame Judge swears her in, "Do you, Mrs. Bobolini, swear to tell the truth so help you God?"

"Of course I do. I'm Catholic." Mrs. Bobolini sits and crosses her sexy legs, raising her skirt a few inches above the knee as she throws a sly glance toward the Jury. No torn stocking this time around.

"So?", asks Madame Judge.

"We always tell the truth."

"Well, we shall see what we shall see. Begin.", orders the Judge.

The Prosecutor steps up. "Mrs. Bobolini, you claim to have suffered abuse at the hands of your -- and I'm quoting you now -- *'lousy, stinking, rotten, wife-beating, beer-drinking, cartoon-watching husband'* that led you to take a knife and slice the top banana. Is that true?"

"I thought it was a wiener.", she says.

"Yes, of course, the wiener."

"It's true. He abused me. He hit me; he hit me hard. Many times and then he bind me ... beat me ... punched me ... humiliated me ... ripped out the finger and toenails ... stripped me of all human dignity ..." then, breathing heavily, she screams ... "RIDE 'EM COWBOY!, he said ..."

Oh, come on, again with the stupid horse whinny? Really?

"... All in the name of matrimonial obligation. So I played Zorro ... and whoosh, wiener no more. I drove quickly from the house. I threw it out the window of my car. It landed in a field next to some cows. I don't know. I drove very fast. And so, now I am here accused of man hating." She sobs now even harder than last time. There goes the mascara again. What a mess. "I am innocent, I tell you. Innocent!"

"Oh, give it a rest, Mrs. Bobolini", the Prosecutor spews, "we've heard your kind of sob story before. Poor me, I'm innocent. He hurt me first. I mean, do you really expect us to believe that?"

"Sure. Why not?"

Up pops the Defense Attorney, playing to the Jury. No dummy this guy, "Exactly. Why not? Why not believe this innocent child? The mother of his children, the cooker of his meals, the washer of his clothes, the cleaner of his house, the Lolita to his Humbert?"

The spectators like this little rat apparently as they all agree "Yeah, that's right ... yeah."

But Madame Judge tells them to shut up. She bangs her gavel furiously. "Quiet! This court will now consider the evidence before it. I am instructing the jury to go forth and find the truth. Now go!"

It seems like there should be more to this trial then there was. The Judge didn't question General Schnitzkof but what more could he have added to Officer WingWing's testimony since the General was on the phone with his commanding officer at the time WingWing found the top banana so to speak. In any case, the jury exited when ordered to do so, because that's what juries do. Thankfully none of them fell on their face when they left the jury box.

"General Schnitzkof", whispers WingWing, "do you think she'll be found guilty?

"Now, how the hell should I know, WingWing? All I know is that there's a wiener in a baggy over there."

"But he deserved it, right, General? I mean he deserved it, like you said. Being mean and all that. He should get the chair ... or, or maybe ... he should be ... well ... hung."

"Under the circumstances, WingWing, I think that's quite out of the question just now."

"Huh? Oh ... yeah.", he giggles.

And nearly just as quickly as they left, it seems, the jurors make their way back into the courtroom. The spectators are all abuzz, whispering their "Ooohs, ahhs ... Oh my goodness, do you think she did it?"

Madame Judge can't stand the racket. She bangs her gavel. It's quite deafening.

"This is very significant, WingWing.", says Schnitzkof, "I feel we are about to see history in the making."

"Has the jury reached a verdict?", asks the Judge.

The Foreman of the jury rises solemnly, then reaches deep into his pocket to remove a crumpled up, coffee and food stained verdict sheet. A piece of bacon falls to the floor. "Yes, Madame Judge. We find the defendant guilty of liberating the wiener but it is also our finding that it was well deserved and we respectfully ask the court for mercy on the part of the defendant who acted in the only manner possible given the disgusting and vile circumstances described earlier."

"So be it. It is the decision of this court ..."

Okay, if you didn't think it was going to happen again, you were wrong. MUSIC ... here it comes. Well, not exactly music, but a drum roll.

"... that Mrs. Bobolini will serve time ..."

And, of course, the drum roll heightens as the Judge continues her sentencing. "In a half-way house ..."

And now a clash of cymbals!

"... supervising druggies and weirdos."

The courtroom spectators erupt, joyously screaming "YAY!", and parade music blares from who the hell knows where.

"In deference to the deed that Mrs. Bobolini has admitted to, I hereby order Mrs. Bobolini to refrain from ever using a knife again. Mrs. Bobolini, do you understand the order of this court?"

"Of course I do, I'm not stupid, you know. I'm just Swedish."

"I thought you were Italian.", says the Judge.

"No, I said I was Catholic."

"Oh. I suppose there's a difference, but this court neither cares nor wishes to hear more on this matter. I hereby dismiss Mrs. Bobolini into the custody of the creeps waiting in the alley where she will be fitted with an anti knife-wielding device. I further rule that Mrs. Bobolini will then be given a rough ride to the county jail where she will spend the first 30-days of her sentence in the slammer to contemplate how she intends to cook without the use of knives. I now declare the marriage of Mrs. Isabella El Marriacchi Bobolini and John Sir Gwaine Bobolini hereby annulled. He can wash his own filthy clothes and cook his own lousy meals and, if he so chooses, he may buy an inflatable doll with which to continue having rough sex. The kids are now up for grabs. Anyone wishing to adopt the damaged goods may apply at the thrift store. This case is now closed!"

BAM goes that gavel one final time.

WingWing turns to Schnitzkof, "So, my General, has justice been served?"

"Well, WingWing, the wiener is nearly back in the pants of its owner and Mrs. Bobolini will never use a knife again and there is no phantom."

WingWing's eyes widen and his head spins about like Linda Blair's in 'The Exorcist' in expectation of the mysterious Phantom Music or, at the very least, the horrible wild windy draft, but nothing happens this time. Relieved, WingWing stands as tall as this little runt can and he and the General exit the courtroom.

"The case is closed, my little nutsack. Life is good. You should be proud."

"I am, my General. Justice has triumphed and life is good."

The jurors and spectators exit the courtroom all overjoyed that the 'Trial of the Century' is over once and for all, or at least until there is another one.

CASE CLOSED.

Yes, life IS good. I got my story!

I looked around the newspaper office to see if there might be other exceptionally tall tales about Avalon and it's crazy cartoon people and sure enough there's a file at the back of the room as big as a large file cabinet. I immediately sent out this dispatch to my boss at the Times Tribune Post in Upper America:

Mystery town discovered. STOP

Crazy cartoon people. STOP

Sending report and case file. STOP

I did a quick look through the other files and, well, all I can say is this place is a goldmine for a reporter.

I grabbed a cuppa joe then took a nap. I knew I needed to be on my toes in the event the crazy weather and even stranger cartoon people blew in.

PART 3

DISPATCH FROM AVALON

Cartoon Town Seeks to
Establish Coffee Empire

AVALON — I've been in this lost community of Avalon in Middle America for roughly two weeks now, hiding out in the town's newspaper office. I dare not go outside as I would attract too much attention from the town's locals, those cartoon people I told you about. This odd species seemed quite taken aback by my appearance, being human as I am, so much so that whenever they saw me milling about town, they stopped dead in their tracks and threw rotten produce at me. Some even spit at me. They threatened to rip out my hair and color me bubble gum pink. I heard they towed my car to the edge of a cliff and pushed it over.

I was nearly starving and thirsting to death when Crispin Murtaugh, the elderly editor of the venerable Avalon Press, found me huddling wretchedly under a staircase and came to my rescue. He's allowing me to stay in the root cellar of the newspaper office where he set up a cot for me to sleep on and he brings food and water daily. I'm surprised that I can even survive on this cartoon food but I guess it's no different from the cardboard junk food and sodas I've been living on all these years. The gummy bears are particularly tasty. They make them with salty sea water, kinda like salt water taffy without the taffy. I just haven't been able to find where the ocean is around here.

Crispin says I'm free to stay here forever as he could use all the help he can get with the case files of the Avalon Defense Department that he's been organizing over the past 50 years.

I like Crispin but I'm certain that forever is too long. I still want to get to Upper America, where I was going before becoming stranded in Avalon. I was on my way there to receive a Pulitzer Prize for a story I did about the Ebola virus when I was embedded with foreign aid workers in West Arica. They're all dead now. I was sick for a short time but got better after drinking some extra strong coffee. You know how coffee is always good for you until it's not? They might want to rethink that. Coffee is always good for something. I even use it as a facial scrub. I know some people like to do coffee enemas to stay healthy but shoving coffee grounds up my butt isn't on my bucket list.

I know I can learn all there is to learn about Avalon by talking to Crispin, occasionally staring out the window and reading the case files of the Avalon Defense Department. General Schnitzkof and Officer WingWing appear to have their thumbs on the pulse of the community.

Speaking of the community and coffee, Crispin tells me that Avalon is soon going to be growing and roasting its own. He says they get so much rain in Avalon and, if they plant the coffee bushes on that cliff overlooking the town from where they pushed my car off, the elevation will be sufficient to create a delectable bean that all the stray cats will want to eat then poop out, the way those Indonesian civet cats do. That way the coffee makers can create an extra pungently strong bean to brew that will also serve as a laxative.

Crispin Protected Me When I
Foolishly Visited The French Quarter

They'll use the proceeds to build the town's first miniature golf and go-kart course.

I'm glad that the coffee Crispin is serving me currently comes from a can.

You may find it interesting to learn that all the food they have here is grown locally in the County of Ligature-Upon-Avon. They don't import anything. So I asked Crispin how they get their canned coffee since they don't yet have a coffee bean industry and he told me that it's simply left on the doorstep of their City Hall each week on a Friday at precisely 5 o'clock in the morning. I'll have to keep my eye out for the next delivery to see what's going on and who's doing what. Maybe it's not really coffee at all. Perhaps it's that fake shit they pass off as coffee - ground chicory, barley, wheat, bran, soy nuggets - you know all that genetically modified crap - or whatever the hell else is in it. I hear the Mormons like it. Of course, if it were the fake stuff, I'd be able to tell. I'll just keep my eye out and let you know.

Since all my luggage was in my car when they sent it over that cliff, I've had to wash my clothes in Crispin's cellar sink which is pretty hard to do with bluejeans. It takes them a full three days to dry so I've had to walk around with newspaper wrapped around me from the waist down. I wouldn't mind so much but all that ink on me makes me look like Guy Pearce in that movie 'Memento' where he was tattooed from head to toe. I liked that movie, by the way.

Speaking of movies, the only ones they show at the Avalon Movie Theater are 'Pipperschniddle', about a little boy who befriends a cockroach and teaches him to dance and 'Peenie' about a girl who grows a penis in her garden and then transplants it onto the back of her pet mouse. The latter one is rated 'X', for mature adults, as you can imagine. Crispin tells me they were both produced in Avalon by a guy named David Crockenburger who died after contracting some cockamamie cockroach disease. That's why they don't have any more movies to show. I told Crispin that I produced and directed my own short film once (at least so far) and maybe, if I offered my services to the townspeople, they'd stop threatening to pull my hair out and paint me bubble gum pink. He said he doubted it.

I discovered another fascinating case from the voluminous case files of the Avalon Defense Department, a.k.a. police department. This one is called 'THE CASE OF THE MISSING HAUNTED MOBILE HOME'.

I didn't know that they have mobile homes in Avalon, but Crispin assured me they do. He said the owners like to wheel them around to change the view from time to time. I wonder if they get hit by tornadoes since the weather is so crazy here in Avalon. I know in Upper America, tornadoes seem to aim for mobile homes in trailer parks. In fact, I'm willing to bet that if we got rid of all the trailer parks, we wouldn't have any tornadoes. Anyway, this really is a humdinger of a case. I found it under the cat litter box that Crispin keeps to catch rats.

PART 4

The Case

of the

Missing Haunted Mobile Home

IT BEGINS one dark and rainy night as so many of these tales tend to do because it rains so much in Avalon. On the other hand, there are quite a few sunshiny days, so there will most likely be a goodly number of crimes perpetrated during the daytime. But for now, this one begins at night ... in the dark ... in the rain ... raining cats and dogs. A few of them even float down into the sewers where the dog catchers and other animal wranglers work overtime. Needless to say, which really means it's so obvious that I need not say it, it is very wet.

Townspeople are rushing to get home from their various boring jobs. Some are drenched to the skin as they wait for the Number 1 Bus, the Avalon Express (as opposed to the Avalon Press which is a newspaper), the only bus operating in Avalon. Some ugly man is out walking his equally ugly little dog. He doesn't even have the common sense to put on a raincoat but his ugly pet is wearing an umbrella strapped to its head. It falls off as soon as the dog trots to keep up.

Then, as it always does, the rain comes to an abrupt halt and the whole town brightens for a split second. But as soon as everyone looks to the skies for confirmation that the wretched rain is indeed over, it starts up again and they all get a good drink.

A moment later it turns even darker and stormier causing people to scatter like rats and then they too float into the sewers. The people at the bus stop churn away like a whipped up whirlpool before disappearing into the dark tunnels beneath the town. Good riddance I like to say. If they can't afford a car, they shouldn't be on the street.

General Schnitzkof and his trusted assistant WingWing are on patrol in their Police Car, that's Car 54, of course. The windshield wipers are going full bore, swishing so fast it'd make your head spin.

The General's trying desperately to see through the heavily fogged window as WingWing grabs bits from a bag of M&Ms, one of his favorites. But for some reason this night, he is only trying to pick out the yellow ones, perhaps because it's so dark those are the only ones he can see.

Then suddenly, loud staticky static comes over the police radio. It's the station's only female dispatcher, Myrtle, "Car 54, we've just got a 1040 call from 90210 Nut Blvd. Can you respond?"

"That's a roger, there, old, girl.", says Schnitzkof, "We're on our way.". The General then turns on the police siren which wails full-on causing WingWing to quickly wrap up his M&Ms bag and shove it in the glove box.

"Gee, General Schnitzkof, what's a 1040? I never heard of that one before."

"It means someone's in trouble."

"I kinda figured that out, oh General of mine. But what kind of trouble?"

"My, my, my ... you're all questions tonight, little WingWing."

"But, General, you always told me to ask questions so that I might learn."

"True, my little flat-footed, round friend. But, right now, I'm trying to remember for myself what 1040 means. It's obviously been a long time since I answered a 1040. It sounds serious, though, wouldn't you agree, WingWing?"

"Oh, for sure. My heart is racing just thinking that maybe there was a horrible, deadly car accident with lots of decapitations."

"No, that's a 1010."

"Or a holdup of a convenience store with bullet riddled bodies on the floor with tongues hanging out?"

"That's a 1020.", reminds Schnitzkof.

"A rabid mad dog foaming at the mouth with ITS tongue hanging out?"

"No, no no. That's a 1030."

"Or a haunted mobile home with ghosts running around the cellar and attic, a dismembered body dangling from the balcony and white sheets that look like strange ugly people, with horrible loud pounding noises like somebody wants to get into the bathroom while you're on the pot, and mysterious winds that gush through the hallways, lifting up your underwear and causing them to lodge in the crack. With lots of people around looking at you so you can't pull them out?

"That's it, WingWing, you've got it! I should have remembered that myself. I answered a 1040 once but that was many moons ago when I was a young round lad like yourself. How time flies, WingWing."

"Yes, General. Time flies."

"Of course, I've never seen it walk.", ponders Schnitzkof.

"Excuse me, Sir?"

"Time, WingWing, time! It never walks. It always flies. Have you never noticed that?"

"I don't think I ever thought about it. But I'm sure if I did, I would notice that it never walked."

"Now you're talking, WingWing. Just you pay attention in the future."

"I promise, Sir. I will keep my ears and eyes open. Look, the rain, it's stopping."

Sure enough, the rain has indeed slowed to a noodle of a trickle as Car 54 rolls up to 90210 Nut Blvd.

"Thank goodness we won't have to listen to that wretched racket any more.", says Schnitzkof, as he screeches his car to a halt.

He and WingWing exit.

In this quaint but a little bit rundown neighborhood there's lots of unusual commotion as bystanders mill about the sidewalk and street. Something's not right here because there's an empty spot where a house used to be.

"What the hell is going on here?", the General blares, "What are all you people doing in the street? Clear the way, clear the way. My word, WingWing. There's nothing there."

Bystanders clear a path for Avalon's top investigators to plow through.

"I see, my General. There's nothing there where there should be something there. It's gone. The house is gone. All the other houses are still there."

"Well, it was a mobile home, WingWing. But still, it's supposed to be there. I mean someone saw it. Someone called in the report. Someone must know something."

Schnitzkof spots an ugly girl on the sidewalk. "You there, you ... yes, the ugly girl with the yellow teeth, purple splotched skin and hideous pimple on her nose and carrying that broom. You. Tell me, have you seen which way the house went?"

In her very ugly voice, the ugly girl responds, "I think it went North. But it could have gone South. I was looking in the mirror at the time."

The ugly girl then walks off toward the empty lot.

"My word, WingWing, are the two of you related by any chance?"

"Of course not, General Schnitzkof. I don't have an ugly sister. I don't even have a pretty one. I'm an only child."

"I suspected as much."

And instantly, there are giant whooshing sounds of wind and trees rustling and lightning cracks causing the bystanders to scream like the idiots they are. They should have stayed home. Then there's a giant THUD and more stupid screaming.

"Ahhhhhh ... ahhhh ... the house is back.", wails a frightened and amazed WingWing, "Look, oh General. It's fallen from the sky ... right onto the ugly girl."

Sure enough, there's the mobile home right where it's supposed to be. It's quite the fixer-upper too.

"Only her legs are still showing", reports WingWing, "and ... look, now they're starting to shrivel up under the house. Oh, yuk! Her shoes, they're red and they're disappearing too."

Now for some reason, even though it seems to happen a lot in Avalon, strange music starts playing. It's 'Somewhere Over the Rainbow'. Such a lovely tune.

"I can see that, WingWing. This is very strange indeed. I knew that ugly girl was in on this. See? Even the house is ugly. You know what they say!"

"No, what do they say?"

"Ducks of a feather, flock together."

"What about water off a duck's back?", WingWing asks innocently.

"Excellent. You're becoming quite the little investigator, my pungent chum. A promotion will soon be in store for you."

"Oh, thank you, Sir. I've been going to night school every morning."

General Schnitzkof is eager to contain the scene of the crime and get on with his investigation. His tugs on his tie, all official like; it means he means business. "Everybody step aside. Off the sidewalk. Now, move!"

There's lots of mumbling and grumbling from the bystanders as they begrudgingly move off the sidewalk and into the street. Then, just as also happens frequently in Avalon, a speeding car shoots by with wheels screeching followed by a loud CLUNK and then a THUD - the sound of a body hitting the ground.

"Oh, oh!", says WingWing.

A body lies grotesquely splattered in the street.

"Better call the coroner, WingWing. All right, everybody, back on the sidewalk but stay out of the way."

More mumbling and grumbling as the bystanders return to the sidewalk.

Almost instantly, an ambulance siren wails and the Coroner's van comes screeching to a halt right where Schnitzkof and WingWing are standing.

"Look, Sir", says WingWing, "it's Dr. Guisseppe."

A serious looking Dr. Guido Guisseppe exits the van and quickly brushes aside the bystanders,

"Get out of my way, you people. I have to investigate a horrible death, I think. Out of my way. Go stand in the street or something."

Again, with the mumbling and grumbling. The Bystanders go back into the street.

"No, Dr. Guisseppe ...", Schnitzkof shouts, "don't ..."

Too late. Another car speeds through with wheels screeching ... followed by a loud CLUNK, then a THUD - another body bites the dust, or in this case, the asphalt.

"All right, everybody who's left, get back on the sidewalk and this time stay out of the way", orders Schnitzkof, "if you know what's good for you."

Exhausted and exasperated, the bystanders again make their way back onto the sidewalk.

"General Schnitzkof, I just heard a report that a house fell on some ugly girl. Thought I'd better check it out for casualties. I see you have a confirmed one in the street there.", says Dr. Guisseppe.

WingWing corrects him, "Two actually."

"Oh dear", says Dr. Guisseppe, "I assume the ugly girl is dead too."

"Dead as a door nail.", announces the General.

"What exactly is a door nail, Sir?", asks WingWing.

"Quiet, WingWing. And, what are you doing wearing those shiny red shoes?"

"I'm not sure, my General. I don't remember putting on any red shoes today."

"They're quite lovely actually.", an admiring Dr. Guisseppe notes, "Especially the little heels. Such sparkle!"; now spotting WingWing's short pants, "My boy, I didn't notice what beautiful legs you have until now. Perhaps we could go for a little ..."

General Schnitzkof quickly interrupts, "Excuse me, Dr. Guisseppe, but I think we'd better get back to matters at hand."

WingWing leans into the General and whispers "Thank you, my General. I owe you one."

"Think nothing of it, WingWing", Schnitzkof whispers back, "Just make sure you use less starch when ironing my undies next time."

"Your wish is my command."

"Now Dr. Guisseppe", says Schnitzkof, "perhaps you'd better scrape the remains from the street of those two Jaywalkers while WingWing and I investigate inside."

"Anything you say, General. Is there anything left of the ugly girl?"

"Perhaps, but you won't be able to extricate her as long as the house is still here. We'll let you know if it disappears again."

"Well, okay, but the body is going to get awfully ripe." Dr. Guisseppe waves away a stinky smell, "If you know what I mean."

"Can't be helped", says the General, "Come along, WingWing."

"Bye, bye, WingWing. I'd be very interested in purchasing a pair of those shoes for myself."

"Run, General Schnitzkof, run." WingWing pushes Schnitzkof toward the front door of the house.

"Well, don't push me, WingWing. I'm moving as fast as I can."

They make their way onto the rickety porch of the mobile home that was missing and now is back and stand at the front door which creaks then opens wide before them.

"Eeeek!", cries WingWing, "The door just opened all by itself."

"It's the wind, little pumpkin lad, have no fear."

But there IS something to fear, especially when the loud GUSH of wind whooshes by.

"Ahhhh ... I'm being pushed inside.", proclaims a shivering WingWing.

They're both pushed into the house by a mysterious force, right into the foyer.

"Me too.", says the General, fighting to remain steadfast, "It's just the wind. It has to be."

"You're right, oh General. Oh, oh, I feel my underwear starting to creep up. Arrgghh!" Why, you can actually hear WingWing's underwear creeping up into his crack. It's fairly disgusting. "Oh, no ... they're still creeping. I hate this. Stop, stop. That's it! Now they're stuck."

"Well, pull them out, for pity's sake."

WingWing pulls out his underwear with a loud POP, "That's better."

Meanwhile here it comes again that haunted music; it's quite low but you can hear it as they stand in the dark foyer. It unnerves WingWing, "This is spooky. It's so dark and dank."

"Not so dark, WingWing. Those shoes are bright enough to light the way."

Sure enough, WingWing's shiny red shoes sparkle, casting a pretty glow as they move deeper into the house. "Well, at least they're good for something.", says a satisfied WingWing.

Inside the mobile home living room, we now see that this is one big old fashioned mansion of a house. A miracle of profound proportions. Some of the furniture are covered with sheets as are the two big mirrors and we see chandeliers swing lightly in the breeze that breezed in from the open front door.

Ghostly sounds wail loudly then continue low which causes a frightened WingWing to let out a little fart. "I'm scared.", he says as he lets out with another pop.

"Don't be.", says Schnitzkof, "There's no such thing as a haunted house. Calm down."

WingWing looks up and spots a large dangling object. "There's something dangling from the balcony."

It's a body!

"You up there. Stop dangling.", demands Schnitzkof, "Come down here this instant and tell us what's been going on in this house. Come down, I say ... why won't it answer, WingWing?"

"Because it has no head."

Yep, it's hanging by its neck, without a head attached. That's a neat trick.

"I see.", Schnitzkof acknowledges grumpily.

Movement in the room catches WingWing's eye, "Oh, no. Here come the white sheets!"

Whooshing sounds as queen-sized sheets fly past them. Schnitzkof's having none of it. "Some kids fooling around, no doubt. I'll just trip them as they go by and we shall see what we shall see."

"Oh, General, I don't mean to be the bearer of bad news. But one of those sheets just ran right through you. Aaaaaaaahhhhh!!!!! I'm out of here!"

WingWing pads quickly away and Schnitzkof is just barely able to grab hold of the back of his shirt. "Not so fast, my little Ratmuffin. Wait for me. Aaaaaahhhhh!"

Schnitzkof and WingWing speed through the house. They make it as far as the foyer where Dr. Guisseppe's appearance stops them dead in their tracks. "What's all the commotion about? The banging and yelling. Did you find more bodies inside?", he asks.

"Ghosts, Dr. Guisseppe, many horrible ghosts.", cries a terrified Wing Wing.

"Were they beautifully naked?"

"They were wearing sheets."

"I'm afraid, he's right Dr. Guisseppe, the house is filled with horrible ghosts. We shall have to call an exterminator.", announces Schnitzkof.

Dr. Guisseppe thinks a moment, "In the old country we would have called a seance. Talk to them and see what's troubling them. By daylight they were always gone."

"Where to?", Wing Wing asks in awe.

"Who cares?", answers Dr. Guisseppe.

"Well, I wouldn't want them showing up at my door!"

"The lad is right.", barks the General, "We must remove them from the house and make sure they never return."

"In that case, you must first have a seance to draw them out and then bring in a priest to exorcise their spirits."

WingWing ponders, "Don't we have to send them to a gym for that?"

"No, no, no ...", Schnitzkof scolds, "ex-OR-cise not ex-ER-cise."

"I'm afraid I don't see the difference.", says poor muddle-headed WingWing.

"Well never mind then", says the General, "there will come a day when you will grow bright and strong and life will no longer be such a mystery to you."

The thought delights WingWing no end, "I can't wait!"

General Schnitzkof now turns his attention to the good doctor, "How do we proceed, Dr. Guisseppe?"

"Have no fear, Dr. Guisseppe, is here!" as he leads them out the front door.

WingWing chuckles, "He made a rhyme. He's very good at that."

They all stop on the front porch of the haunted mobile home and Dr. Guisseppe looks around. "First we need to find a psychic to conduct the seance."

He scans the crowd of bystanders who are still hanging around and spots a craggy old psychic. "You there, you ... the woman wearing the turban and sandals, the one carrying the crystal ball and tarot cards. Yes, you. Are you a psychic?"

The Psychic approaches them warily, then in a thick Hungarian accent says, "Of course I'm a psychic. Don't I look like a psychic? I mean, I got the crystal ball right here. You think I'd be carrying around this stupid ball if I weren't a psychic? See, my shop's right across the street."

She points to a little house across the street which has a big neon sign 'PSYCHIC'. "See, the sign? It says 'Psychic'. You want I should take you there? You want I should read your palm, maybe?

You want I should read your tea leaves, maybe? You want I should read your tarot cards? You need some kind of proof ... some kind of guarantee that you'll be married and have a bunch of ugly little brat kids or something?"

"Could you?", giggles WingWing.

Schnitzkof seems suspicious. He leans into Dr. Guisseppe and whispers "I see we shall have to negotiate for her services." He then turns to the Psychic, "Listen you Psychic, you, we'll give you five dollars to conduct a seance for us at the ugly house."

"Five dollars? A pox on you!"

"Guzundtheit!" says WingWing.

"Who is this moronic moron in uniform?" demands an annoyed Psychic.

"That is WingWing, my trusted assistant. And I'll thank you not call him a moronic moron. I can do that myself."

"I said a POX on you!", she announces even louder.

"Oh, a POX.", says WingWing, "What's a pox?"

"That means she just cursed us with smallpox.", says Dr. Guisseppe

"Smallpox? Aaaaaahhhh!", cries WingWing.

"Don't be silly, WingWing. She can't do that.", sighs the General.

"Hold on a minute." Guisseppe looks closely at WingWing's face. One by one red dots erupt. "What are those little red spots appearing on your face, WingWing?"

"A rash?"

"Of course. Continue, General Schnitzkof."

"Well, what will it be, Psychic?"

"Twenty dollars and not a penny less."

"Done!"

Guisseppe leans in whispering "Good for you General. You handled that quite nicely."

Whispering back, "Yes, I did, didn't I?"

"Now we need a Priest." says Guisseppe. He glances around the crowd and spots a man milling about. "Hey, you ... yes, you ... the man wearing the black robe and funny hat, with the little white collar, carrying those glass beads and molesting that altar boy. Yes, you. Are you a Priest?"

"Of course I'm a Priest. Don't I look like a Priest? You think I'd be dressed like this, carrying around these stupid glass beads and molesting this altar boy if I weren't a Priest?"

The Priest points out his little Church, which is a few doors down from the Psychic's house. It sports an oversized neon cross. "See, my Church is right across the street. See, the sign? You want I should take you there? You want I should say mass, maybe? You want I should light some candles? You want I should hear your confession? You need some kind of proof ... some kind of guarantee that you'll go to heaven in the not too distant future?"

"Could you?", asks WingWing hopefully.

"Who is this moronic moron in uniform?"

"This is ... oh never mind.", says Schnitzkof, "Listen, Priest, we'll give you five dollars for the poor box if you'll conduct an exorcism for us at the ugly house."

"Fifty dollars and not a penny less!"

"Done!", yells Guisseppe.

Schnitzkof whispers to the doc, "What ... are you crazy, fifty dollars?"

"You said you wanted the ghosts gone, didn't you? Well it's gonna cost you. Besides, who you gonna call?"

The musical strains of 'Ghostbusters' whistles through. Hear it? Well, never mind if you didn't. Just pretend you did. This is a book. You're supposed to use your imagination. Try a little harder next time. Oh, you say, you never saw 'Ghostbusters', so you don't know what the theme song sounds like? Well that's a poor excuse. Moving on ...

"Of course, you're right, Dr. Guisseppe. All right, everybody, let's go back inside the ugly house and kick some butt."

The General, WingWing, Dr. Guisseppe, the Psychic and the Priest all move toward the door of the haunted mobile home. And once again, the door creaks its creaky creaking sounds and then there's a loud GUSH of wind.

"Aaaaahhhhh. We're being pulled inside again." says Schnitzkof as he fights to maintain composure.

That damn haunted music again and ghostly wailing sounds.

Our trusty clan has been pulled into the foyer. And another gush of wind rams them hard from behind. WingWing whimpers, "Here comes the wind again. Oh no ... they're starting to creep up again. My underwear. It's starting all over again."

"Yes, mine too.", says Schnitzkof.

"Oooooppps", howls Guisseppe, "There she goes."

And the Psychic, "Yes, I feel it too. Nasty thing this wind."

But the Priest confesses, "I'm not wearing any underwear."

"Wingwing, if you let me help you pull them out, you can help me."

"That's okay, Dr. Guisseppe, I've already taken care of it. Thank you."

"Well, perhaps next time."

"All right, everyone, we're wasting time.", hisses Schnitzkof, "Let's get this seance on the road. Where do you want us, Psychic?"

"Under the dangling body would be nice."

"So be it.", orders Schnitzkof, "Everybody under the dangling body. You're sure it won't fall on any of us?" There's lots of commotion as they all stumble around in the dark toward the dangling body.

"No, they only dangle. They don't fall."

They're each bumping into the other and everyone but the Psychic becomes startled when some candles magically light up. The Psychic then motions for everyone to take a seat at the big round table that just happens to be there. Schnitzkof, of course, sits beside his trusted companion WingWing who gets stuck sitting right next to the Psychic who asks "Is everybody ready? They mumble in acknowledgment. "Okay, let's all hold hands.", she says.

They follow the Psychic's command and clasp hands. "General, I wonder if I might switch places with you and sit next to WingWing.", Guisseppe asks gingerly.

WingWing stiffens, whispers whimperingly "No, General, don't."

"I'm afraid not, Dr. Guisseppe, you see, we're bonded, the little pumpkin lad and myself. We go back a long ways."

"I see. I didn't realize there was something between you. I won't interfere again. But he is very cute, you know."

"Yes he is."

"Thank you, my General", whispers the little pumpkin lad, "I owe you another one."

"Never fear, my little trusted companion. Just make sure you remember to sew those little red hearts on my socks like you promised."

"Oh, for sure, Sir."

Now with a harsh look, Schnitzkof says "Come on Psychic. Time is of the essence."

The Psychic adjusts her turban and straightens up in her chair, "I shall now begin", then pauses a moment for full effect before continuing, "Oh spirits of the western world. Oh spirits of the eastern world. Oh spirits of the northern world. Oh spirits of the southern world. Are you there?"

Dead silence.

"I said ... are you there?"

Not a peep.

"You'd better answer me, you stupid spirits."

The Psychic cocks her head, desperate to hear any sounds at all. Absolute silence, not even a flicker from one of the flickering candles. "Hey, I'm starting to lose my patience, now.", she screams,

"Answer me or I'll curse you to hell for the rest of your lives.

"They're dead.", reminds WingWing.

"The rest of your dead lives.", she adds.

Then all of a sudden there are loud banging noises and the table rocks violently.

"Ah Ha! I knew they couldn't deny my command. So what the hell is wrong with you guys, anyway? You got some kinda gripe against the neighborhood or something. Someone maybe done you wrong? Knock twice if you got something to say."

There are two loud knocks coming from the table.

Schnitzkof is excited. "We're getting closer. Ask them if anyone has been horribly murdered in the house and if they're trying to avenge the death. That's always a good reason for a haunting."

"Now, how the hell would you know? You talk to the dead a lot?" The Psychic explodes, "You wouldn't be trying to tell me my job, now would you?"

"Heavens no!"

"Good.", the Psychic then continues, "So you guys up there ... was one of you horribly murdered in this house and are you now trying to avenge the death? Knock once if that's the case."

One loud knock.

"Ah ha!, Schnitzkof says, "Ask them who it is."

"How the hell can I ask them who it is? You got a list of names or something?"

"No. Well ... can't they talk?", asks the General, "They always manage to talk in the movies."

"Okay, okay. But it's gonna cost ya. Fifty bucks to make them talk."

"Done!", shouts Dr. Guisseppe.

"Are you crazy?", whispers Schnitzkof.

"You want the case solved, right? Well, you have to get the ghosts to name names. There's no two ways about it.", explains the Doc.

"All right.", says Schnitzkof begrudgingly, "Proceed, Psychic."

"Everybody hold hands tightly and don't let go no matter what happens. Otherwise you might break the spell. That goes doubly for you, Priest.", as the Psychic glares at him, "And triple for the little moron. No one breaks the circle."

WingWing whispers "I'm getting scared, oh General."

"Hold on tight little chum. I'll protect you."

"I'm holding, oh General. I won't let you down."

Ghostly wailing sounds pick up along with the tinkling of glass and the table literally bounces up and down while another loud gush of wind sails on in.

"Oh, no, they're coming.", wails WingWing.

"That's for sure. With bells on.", roars Dr. Guisseppe.

"I don't hear any bells.", says WingWing who listens intently until, sure enough, bells ring.

"There they are.", acknowledges Guisseppe.

The Priest, who's been patient up till now, starts to wiggle in his seat, "Hurry up, already. I have to say mass in about an hour."

"Hey look, Priest, you'll get your turn in a minute. So just sit back and be quiet.", scolds the snotty Psychic.

"Yeah, yeah.", says the petulant Priest.

Now back on track, the Psychic continues "Okay you guys in spirit land. Hurry up and say what you gotta say. I will now go into a trance. Remember, no one breaks the circle." The Psychic closes her eyes and starts rocking back and forth and side to side.

"This is rather exciting. It reminds me of a little game we used to play in the old country.", says Dr. Guisseppe, "Only then, we called it a daisy chain and everyone was alive. Quite alive, if you catch my meaning."

"I don't", says WingWing, "but perhaps you could ..."

Schnitzkof clasps a hand over WingWing's mouth.

"Hmm, hmmmm.", WingWing struggles.

"Trust me, WingWing, you don't want to know."

The Psychic opens one eye, staring down Schnitzkof which cues him to reclasp Guisseppe's hand.

Back in form, the Psychic continues, "Quiet. I am now entering my trance ... Hear me oh spirits from around the globe. Speak your peace or forever hold it. Who's dead up there and how did it happen and what the hell do you want us to do about it?"

There's horrible wailing sounds and more pounding on the table then glass tinkling followed by several loud lightning cracks. From the Psychic come spooky slobbering garbled noises followed by more ghostly screaming low and then high.

"Aaahhhhh, the ghost is coming.", WingWing proclaims. "Hold tight, hold tight. Don't let go."

The General tightens his grip on WingWing's hand. "Stay strong, little pea pod."

"Holy canoli. I'M coming, I'M coming.", blares Guisseppe.

"Is HE the ghost, oh General?", WingWing asks innocently.

"I think he may be talking about something else. Close your ears."

Just then, the table rattles wildly and spins like a top then abruptly stops. A strange eerie voice wails horribly from the rafters. It's the Ghost!

"My name is Harvey Harold Irving Weinstein." Chains rattle loudly causing everyone to shiver. "I was killed twenty-five years ago on my birthday. They killed me ... stabbed me ... shot me through and through then hanged me from the balcony after cutting off my head and staking it in the garden."

Schnitzkof wrinkles his nose in disgust. "Yeech.

"I don't remember seeing any head in the garden.", responds Guisseppe.

"The chickies ate my head long ago."

Guisseppe's eyes twinkle, "This is very similar to the game we once played."

"I want my death avenged!", shouts the Ghost amid horrible wailing and chain rattling.

"Who killed you, ghost ... er, I mean, Mr. Weinstein?" asks Schnitzkof.

"My audience."

"I'm afraid I don't understand."

"That's the trouble. No one understands.", the Ghost wails and cries "boo-hoo, woe is me, woe is me."

"What do you mean your audience killed you?", asks Schnitzkof.

"They couldn't take a joke, so they killed me. I was a stand-up comedian."

"Not a very good one, I imagine.", hisses Guisseppe.

"I heard that. God will get you for that ... and your little dog too."

"This is not a dog. This is the General's most trusted assistant, WingWing."

"Oh."

"Wait a minute", interrupts Schnitzkof, "I find it very hard to believe that an audience would come to this house to see a show."

"The house used to be located in the Catskills. I was the star attraction at Marcie and Merv's Catskill Holiday Resort and Gefilte Fish Deli."

Wait a minute. Are we to believe that cartoon people could have been living in Catskills, New York in Upper America and no one ever noticed? Yes! They'll let anyone in.

Schnitzkof sputters, "Well, unless you know the names of the entire audience that killed you...",

Instantly, an endless stream of paper wafts down from the balcony and lands on the table.

"Here's the list."

Schnitzkof quickly scans the paper. "I don't see any names on this paper. The names must have faded over the years."

The poor Ghost is bereft. He wails and rattles his chains incessantly, "Woe is me."

Irritated by the whole affair, the Priest finally speaks up, "Hey, Psychic, your time is up. Let me get rid of this guy ... would someone please wake up the Psychic."

By now, the Psychic looks like a lunatic rabid bat slobbering all over herself. Her tongue's hanging out and she's foaming at the mouth.

"I can't.", WingWing cries, "She's rigid like a rod."

The Priest shakes his rosary beads at the Ghost. "Beware, Ghost, the forces of evil cannot take this vile, pitiful, frothy-mouthed woman from this earth. I shall cast you out of this ugly house, you and your ugly dead, decapitated body and any of your ugly friends who may be hanging around."

The Ghost wails ever louder.

"In the name of the father ... in the name of the son ... in the name of the holy ghost...."

"I'M the ghost!", shouts the ghost.

"I cast you out. I cast you out."

"What about the audience? My murderers."

"If you don't get out of here, you ghost, we just might murder you a second time.", warns Guisseppe.

"Out, oh dead ugly spirit." continues the Priest, "Out....damn spot ... out ..."

Everyone but the crazed half conscious Psychic takes to chanting, "Out ... out ... out."

They pause a moment then begin again, "Out ... out ... out!"

"Is he out yet, my General?"

Glass tinkles; the table wobbles; there's the seemingly endless pounding and loud wailing ... then it gets lower and lower ... until ...

"I think he's going.", says Schnitzkof.

"Is that it?", asks Guisseppe, "What a pitiful ghost, indeed. I thought we'd at least go for another hour or so."

"I don't get paid by the hour. I get paid by the job. He's gone and you owe me fifty bucks.", says the Priest, "Now pay up."

Schnitzkof looks over to WingWing, "WingWing give him the money."

The Priest pulls out a pen and writes up a pretty extensive bill for his services.

"But I don't have any money. I spent the last on the donuts.", admits WingWing.

Schnitzkof whispers, "What about you, Dr. Guisseppe, you have some money?"

"Don't look at me. I'm as broke as a bloke."

WingWing whispers excitedly "Look, look General, the Psychic is starting to wake up. I bet she has some money."

"But we owe her too."

"Let's steal her money and tell her the ghost took it when she was in the trance.", says WingWing.

"What would a ghost want with money?" Schnitzkof asks.

"Maybe to buy some head?", says WingWing.

"Hmmm. You may be right. Go steal her money."

"Well, okay, but you be the lookout."

WingWing pads around the table and pilfers through the Psychic's pocket just as she groggily comes to "Wa? Wa? What happened? What's going on?"

"Nothing.", says WingWing, as he quickly pulls his hands away. He then passes a wad of bills to Schnitzkof who hands the Priest his due.

"Here's your fifty, Priest. Thank you for your help. Now let's everybody get out of here."

They begin exiting their seats.

"So is the beastly ghost gone?", the Psychic says as she slobbers all over herself.

"For sure, oh lady of psych.", says WingWing.

"Good. I'll take my money now."

"But, but ...", WingWing stammers.

Schnitzkof to the rescue, "What the lad is trying to say is ..."

"We paid you your money before you went into the trance", Dr. Guisseppe interrupts, "don't you remember? Of course, you do. But you hit your head on the table and so you probably just forgot. A little bit of amnesia. You'll be fine in no time. Not to worry."

"Hey, what is this? Is this some kinda scam? Are you guys really who you say you are?"

"Of course we are.", snarls an indignant Schnitzkof, "Psychic, you may take to the road. How dare you imply that we are less than honest?"

WingWing jumps to the General's defense, "Yeah, how dare you?"

"Shut up, you little pip-squeak rodent, you little mouse from Munchkinland, you little piece of ..."

"Enough!", screams the General, "The case of the missing haunted mobile home is closed. The ghost is dead."

And with that, they make their way toward the front door, with the Psychic, still half groggy, stumbling after them.

"Long live the ghost!", Guisseppe announces with a salute.

"I thought he was dead.", says WingWing.

"He IS dead. Dead as a door nail.".

"What exactly is a door nail?", asks WingWing.

"Never you mind. I don't.", says the effervescent doc, "Are you sure you won't part with those lovely red shoes?"

Schnitzkof pushes ahead, "The case is closed, WingWing, my little trusted friend. Life is good. You should be proud."

"I am, my General. Justice has triumphed again and life is good."

The troupe exits the no longer haunted mobile home while a big gush of wind follows them out slamming the door behind them.

CASE CLOSED.

Yes, life is good! The forgotten files of the Avalon Defense Department are now coming to light thanks to me.

<u>Note to Editor:</u> Times Tribune Post, Upper America:

Town Coroner is gay (not that there's anything wrong with it). STOP

Need Meteorologist in Avalon ASAP. STOP

Priests molest altar boys here too. STOP

PART 5

DISPATCH FROM AVALON

Crow Attack May Be Tied to Terrorists; Investigation Stalled

AVALON — I said I'd keep you posted about how the canned coffee gets delivered to Avalon when allegedly they don't import anything.

Last week I crept up to Avalon's City Hall at 4:30 in the morning on a Friday in anticipation of the delivery and what I have to report is nothing less than astounding. At 5 a.m. precisely, a large caseload of canned coffee appeared. No truck, no car, no train, no people. Nothing. It was just there when before there was nothing, kind of like the case of the haunted mobile home, only in reverse. I saw it with my own eyes. Crispin was right.

I am beginning to believe that this is indeed the Twilight Zone. Perhaps that's why every time I run to the edge of town I'm right back where I started. Of course that doesn't happen to the cartoon people who live here.

The County of Ligature-Upon-Avon is pretty large for a cartoon county because, from what I've seen of the case files of the Avalon Defense Department, that Crispin has been collecting all these years, there have been strange goings on all around, far and wide and near and far, past and present.

A few weeks ago, Magnolia Winterford Wobbles was out picking cotton on the back 40 of her farm when she was attacked by a swarm of black crows. They ate her eyes out and pecked her to death. This was even though she had no less than 1000 scarecrows positioned throughout her property. It was right after I came to Avalon.

Crispin told me a bunch of the townspeople were blaming me as the source of some strange evil. I assured him I had nothing to do with it because I'm an atheist and we don't believe in anything, God or the Devil. Actually, I think the Devil may really be God, just as God is the Father, the Son and the Holy Ghost. For all I know he may be the Virgin Mary too. If you ask me the whole thing is a bit cracked. Anyway, if they're looking for a culprit, they might want to consider those crazed Islamic terrorists that are spreading like locusts across the desert of mankind. They'll recruit anything that moves.

Crispin said he'd look into it, although, frankly, I'm surprised he didn't consider that for himself.

Of course, it's quite possible that the crows were really drones in disguise, but then they probably would have just shot her to death. Unless, of course, they were designed to mimic the terrible terrorist tactics of the Islamic terrorist crazies. Oh my gosh, did I just say that ... I mean 'extremist terrorists' ... or is it 'terrorist extremists' ... although, aren't all terrorists extremists? ... but then they would have just beheaded her. Unless, of course, they were trying to fool everyone into believing that they had nothing to do with it and that it was really some other source of evil intent on killing poor Magnolia Winterford Wobbles. I guess we'll never know. I just hope the Avalonians leave me out of this. I didn't even know her. What motive would I have had to off her in that monstrously morbid manner?

Magnolia's dipstick daughter Drusilla disappeared on the same day of the cowardly crow attack. I wonder if she left to join the terrorists' cause. According to reports, Drusilla had been wearing a ski mask recently on all her trips to the grocery store and kept a dagger on her belt. No one thought that was strange because everyone knew Drusilla was recently released from the Avalon Looney Bin where she was sent after her father Hatsumoto Loco Wobbles committed Hara-Kiri during a full moon last year on Halloween.

From what I hear, the case of Magnolia's pecking is still wide open and the Avalon Defense Department is contemplating whether or not to investigate. They're waiting on Dr. Guisseppe's findings. That could take a while. Dr. Guisseppe is very thorough. I remember, after I read the Case of the Missing Member report, Crispin told me that the good doctor had taken extra special care and time in sizing up the sliced-off 'top banana' belonging to John Sir Gwaine Bobolini. And when it came time to reattaching it, Dr. Guisseppe volunteered to do the surgery at no cost as long as he was permitted to make a plastic mold of the Bobolini family jewel once it was fully functional again. He keeps it by his bedside on a little nightstand, I've been told. He had it fashioned into a glow-in-the-dark sucker.

Now from what Crispin tells me, there's been a backlog of late. General Schnitzkof and Officer WingWing got sidetracked from their usual case load when the little rookie's cream puff went missing while they were in the French Quarter.

Crispin filed a Freedom of Information request to get an early copy of the investigation report before its official release to the media. Here it is.

PART 6

The Cream Puff Caper

IT BEGINS on a cheerful sunny day, for a change, in the town of Avalon. Birds flit happily about the trees; balloons and welcoming flags decorate the charming little pastel and jewel hued houses. People greet one another warmly with a tip of the hat, a wink of an eye, a handshake and a slap on the back. Yes, they do all of that in that order.

But for one poor soul, a kid no less, things change in the blink of an eye when a speeding car plows right over him as he crosses the street on his way home from the candy store. His flattened body lay on the center divide, face down. His bag of candy nothing but a pile of melted gum drops and wax lips along with peppermint patties that look like cow plops.

A split second later a Coroner's van arrives at the scene. Avalon's famed County Coroner, Dr. Guido Guisseppe, exits, alternately whistling and humming 'Zippedy Do-Dah'. He uses a shovel to scrape the body into a body bag and hurls it into the back of the van, then zips right out of there, back to the morgue to cut open the kid and sell his organs to the highest bidder.

Everyone else is oblivious to the tragedy because, in Avalon, it only happened if you witnessed it and then it's soon forgotten anyway. In this case, there are no witnesses to the splattering on this fine sunshiny day. At least none who are willing to talk.

The town center is filled with tiny elegant shops and restaurants. People browse windows while others enter or exit the quaint shops, ignoring the old man with an 'Occupy Main Street' sign attached to his walker as he slowly makes his way along the sidewalk.

Oh, listen, there's lovely French Café music playing as he moseys on over to the French Quarter.

The French Quarter is fairly new to Avalon but it's become quite popular of late. Visitors enter through the large archway where it says

'French Quarter', of course, where there are still more quaint shops, cafés and restaurants. All things French including the people. Well, not really. Some are only pretending to be French because they love the sound of the snobbish sexy French accent, all sophisticated and European sounding, and the way they wear those funny berets on their heads and the fact that they like Jerry Lewis when no one else in the free world does.

General Schnitzkof and Officer WingWing are seated at an outdoor table at Monet's French Café. I didn't think the General would be seen dead in the French Quarter, seeing as how he's a die-hard Brit. Nevertheless, Schnitzkof is enjoying his coffee and reading a newspaper while WingWing is just about to dig into a huge cream puff.

Suddenly, WingWing drops the delectable puff back onto the plate. "Oh, no, my General. I have to go potty. That was some fast acting coffee that Chef gave us."

Schnitzkof looks up from his newspaper. "Well don't just sit there crossing your legs and hiney, go inside and ask him to use the bathroom."

"Okay." WingWing bolts, banging the table and chairs, causing silverware to fly off the tables as he rushes past and in through the open door to the café. He runs up to Chef Monet. "Excuse me, oh Chef, but do you have a potty? I need to go potty real bad."

Chef Monet, a huge mustachioed fellow wearing a Chef's hat, is behind his pastry counter laying out some lovely madeleine cookies. He screams loudly in his well practiced French accent "Sacre bleu! Who is this moronic moron in uniform?"

Schnitzkof screams back from his position at the outdoor table, "That's my trusted assistant WingWing. And I'll thank you not to call him a moronic moron. I can do that myself. Just show him to the bathroom."

"Oui, oui, Monsieur General."

WingWing is standing with his legs crossed and hands shaking in agony. "No, not wee-wee, oh Chef. I have to do DOO-DOO."

"Sacre bleu, you mor ... ah, little monsieur ... it's over there."

WingWing makes a dash for the bathroom.

"Sacre bleu! Mon Dieu!" cries Chef Monet, trying calmly to continue his chores despite being distracted by the noises coming from inside the bathroom ... a banging door, various loud farts, the flushing toilet, two more flushes, another banging door then the sink water running and finally ... the exterior door to the bathroom opening and banging shut. BAM!

The Chef jumps from the noise and grabs his hat to keep it from being shaken from his head.

WingWing then flies back through the café and pops up at his outdoor table where Schnitzkof peeks out from behind his newspaper.

"I am back, my General."

"I can see that, little round chum. Do you feel better?"

"Yes, my General. Umm, are you going to finish your coffee?"

"I was thinking about it. But, go ahead."

WingWing reaches for Schnitzkof's coffee when he shrieks suddenly. "Eeeeeeeekkkkkk! My dessert. My cream puff. You ate my cream puff while I was going potty."

Only a few crumbs remain on WingWing's side of the table. Even the plate is gone.

"I did no such thing.", says an indignant Schnitzkof, "You must have eaten it yourself before you went potty."

"No, I didn't. I was saving it. I didn't have time to eat my cream puff. The coffee made me go too fast to have eaten my cream puff. Somebody ate my cream puff and it wasn't me."

"Well, it wasn't me, WingWing. I never touched your cream puff. Are you sure it didn't fall to the floor when you left the table?"

WingWing checks the floor. "It's not on the floor. There's nothing on the floor except some silverware, a few napkins ... a couple of mushrooms ... three wads of gum ... some spit ... and two fish with their heads cut off."

Sure enough, each of these items is on the floor under the table. Schnitzkof bends down to have a look. "What's that on the bottom of your shoe?"

WingWing checks his shoe. "An éclair and some chocolate mousse." Now whining, "I didn't step on any cream puff. I want my cream puff."

"Stop whining.", orders Schnitzkof, "We'll just order you another."

"No, I already picked the biggest cream puff they had. I want MY cream puff back."

"WingWing, you're beginning to make a scene. The Chef is going to get angry and kick us out."

Chef Monet is glaring out the window from his position behind the pastry counter.

"I bet HE stole my cream puff just so he could put it back in the case and sell it to somebody else. He doesn't like me. I can see it in his eyes."

"Don't be silly, WingWing. No one likes you."

"Oh."

"Okay, my little cabbage head, I'll help you find your cream puff ... or my name isn't General Schnitzkof." And with that, the General has a coughing fit ... he coughs ... and coughs ... and coughs something disgusting.

"Thank you, my General. I am forever in your debt."

"Yes, well, where would you like to start?"

"I think with the Chef.", says WingWing.

"But he didn't even come over to the table when you were in the potty. How is he a suspect?"

"He made the cream puff, didn't he? Maybe it was a disappearing cream puff."

"Excellent deduction, my boy. You're getting better with each passing day. You'll get to be lieutenant before the year's out."

"Oh, thank you, Sir. I couldn't do it without your guidance. I've taken many notes. See?" WingWing whips out his note pad from his necklace-styled purse.

"Yes, you've become quite the little investigator."

"I'm going to go over and investigate the Chef right now." WingWing quickly makes his way back to the Chef. And here we go again with the banging of table and chairs, the crashing glass and silverware of whatever's left after the first assault.

WingWing now enters the café and approaches the Chef who's muttering under his breath, "Sacre bleu, he's coming back." And now louder, to WingWing, "Aren't you gone yet?"

"Not so fast, Chef, you stole my cream puff. Admit it."

Schnitzkof strides into the café just behind WingWing. "Hold on there, WingWing, that's not how you question a suspect. Let me handle this. Listen, Chef, the little chum here has lost his cream puff while he was in the potty and we were wondering if you might have seen where it went."

"His cream puff? His cream puff? It's probably in his stomach or down the toilet by now. How would I know where his cream puff is?"

"I see you're not the cooperating sort, Chef Monet. Well, we shall see what we shall see. WingWing, look in the case and see if the cream puff is there."

The pastry case is filled with many scrumptious delights, but only two measly looking cream puffs.

"I'm looking, oh General,. It's not there."

"Look in the refrigerator and see if it's hiding in there."

WingWing rushes behind the counter and rifles through the refrigerator, pushing aside gigantic cartons of milk, cream and eggs and ton-like bricks of butter. No Cream Puff. He feverishly arrives back in front of the counter puffing hard from his exertion.

"It's not there either.", he puffs.

"Well then, it's obviously not the Chef. We shall have to look elsewhere.", reports Schnitzkof.

The General looks around inside the café, then spots a lone patron. "You, you there, the man sitting at that table by the window, eating that fish head, yes you. Did you see or have you ever seen this round lad's cream puff?"

The fish eater spews a slew of French sounding curses at them.

"What did he say, oh General?"

"Suffice it to say ... he's not our man."

"Oh. Well, where does that leave us and my cream puff now?"

"I'm not sure, little tadpole. Perhaps the perpetrator has left the premises and we must look far and wide. Why, the cream puff could be anywhere by now ... if it's still alive."

WingWing is horrified. "We must find it, General. There's been a horrible injustice and crime done."

"Let's go", orders Schnitzkof, "There's no time to lose. There's only a very short window in which to recover a kidnap victim."

WingWing and the General hurriedly exit the café. They stand under the arch, surveying the town beyond The French Quarter. Signs of normalcy everywhere. Then, Schnitzkof sniffs the air. But, for the moment, he's utterly clueless.

"Should we round up the usual suspects?", asks WingWing.

"Excellent! Who's first on the list?"

WingWing pulls out his note pad and pages through it ... "The Maloney Brothers."

Schnitzkof's face pales. His body shivers. Legs grow weak. Giant beads of sweat form on his brow. He sputters, "Ahh ... I ... ahh, don't think .... Ahh ... ahh ..., Oh, ahh ... all right, who's LAST on the list?"

WingWing checks the list again. "Madame Candy."

"To the car!", the General announces with an arm raised high as if he's just signaled the Charge of the Light Brigade.

WingWing and Schnitzkof trot past the fancy French Quarter arch and hop into their Police Car 54. And with sirens blaring, they drive to the far edge of Main Street where there's another archway and another big sign, this one in lipstick red neon. It says 'Red Light District'!

They walk through the archway and into the alley where sexy and sleazy sex shops dot either side of the dim but light speckled walkway. There is an interesting array of posed mannequins, both human and animal, sexy clothing and adult toys filling the shop windows. A giant blown up condom waves 'Welcome' above one shop while a life-size dildo with a happy face stands erect outside another. Odd looking patrons of all sorts move in an out of shops and at the back end of the alley is Madame Candy's, an elegantly seedy two-story Brothel.

Working girls hang out on the balcony giggling and smoking while one rides a mechanical bull. One of them spots WingWing and tosses a large string of beads at him. The beads fall over and down his rotund little body, landing at his ankles. He takes two steps and falls flat on his face.

Without missing a beat, Schnitzkof scoops him back up and pockets the beads.

Upon reaching the front door, Schnitzkof tells WingWing "Perhaps you'd better wait here." He then enters alone, leaving WingWing to stand around awkwardly.

One of the younger balcony ladies, a freckle-faced Mirabelle, with bows holding back long yellow pigtails, blows kisses down at WingWing as he waits patiently.

Inside Madame Candy's brothel is an elegant old-fashioned waiting room with extravagant Tiffany styled lamps, beaded curtains and lush red velvet chairs and sofas.

And, entering from a back room is Madame Judge, of all people, whom we remember from our first case. She moves brusquely past Schnitzkof who makes like he's tipping his hat to her.

"Madame Judge.", the General acknowledges curtly.

"General Schnitzkof.", says Madame Judge with her triangular face twitching. She passes stiffly and exits, nearly bumping into WingWing, who's now giggling and blowing kisses up to Mirabelle. The Judge pauses, thinks better of it and moves quickly off, unseen by WingWing.

Back inside the brothel, Schnitzkof has snuggly planted himself in one of the overstuffed chairs. He rises as Madame Candy, a large buxom professional

Madame Candy
General Schnitzkof's Main Squeeze

in 'barely-there' wear, makes her entrance, clicking through the boudoir styled receiving room in her feathery pink mule slippers with those tiny stupid heels. "Oh, General Schnitzkof, to what DO I owe the pleasure of your company on this fine lovely day?"

Schnitzkof straightens his tie and posture. "Well, Madame Candy, I must tell you that I am here on official police business."

"I see", she says slyly, "that's exactly the kind of business I like. She holds out her hands, playfully, ready to be handcuffed.

Schnitzkof whispers, "Not now, old girl. I mean REAL police business."

Disappointed, Madame Candy fiddles with Schnitzkof's tie before sitting on the sofa. She motions for the General to sit beside her. "Now what's all this about OFFICIAL police business?" She yanks him by the tie right up to her lips and kisses him passionately before falling on top of him.

Schnitzkof struggles to speak with her sloppy kisses and then bobbling breasts in his face. "We've ... mmmm ... incident ... mmmm ... French Quarter ... mmmm".

"How exciting.", chirps Madame Candy, "I love the French. Take me, oh General ... take me now. And take me hard!"

And so he does.

Later, outside the brothel, WingWing is seated on the porch steps playing a game of Jacks. He looks up as Schnitzkof exits adjusting his belt buckle.

"So, my General, did Madame Candy take my cream puff?"

"No, my boy, she had an excellent alibi. It just took me a while to get it out of her. Okay, now, who's next on the list?"

"You want I should keep going from bottom to top?"

"Yes, that's the way I like it."

WingWing curiously watches Schnitzkof fiddle with a shirt button then checks his note pad. "Oh no, Mr. Parabolikos is next."

"Oh dear. He's not going to like seeing us again so soon.", says the General.

They walk back down the alley to the edge of the Red Light District.

"For sure, Sir. The last time he threw his binoculars at us."

"Well, it is what it is. Let's get on with it, then."

"Sir, is it ever NOT what it is?

"Certainly! It can always be something that it's not. That's what you call a parable."

WingWing comes to a stop in front of one of the sex shops. He flips through his note pad and writes the word down as 'Parraball = NOT what it is'.

Meanwhile, Schnitzkof's looking at a sex slave mannequin wearing a dog collar in the window. "Comes from the Greek ... Egads! Parabolikos. That's it! He's not what HE seems."

WingWing looks quizzically at Schnitzkof and then at what he's written. "I don't know, Sir, this word doesn't look right."

Schnitzkof takes a gander at it. "Of course it doesn't look right because it's not what IT seems.

"Thank you, my General, I knew you would set me straight."

"Those damn Greeks", huffs Schnitzkof, "they're always telling stories and they're never what they seem! Golden Fleeces. Trojan Horses. Not worth a spit!"

"You always told me that spitting in public was a disgusting habit never to be done by a civilized person."

"That's true.", says Schnitzkof, "Now, how on earth did we get on this topic, anyway?"

"Mr. Parabolikos", says WingWing.

"Damn that man makes me angry. Let's go!"

Police Car 54, now disguised with a huge inflatable ant on top covering the police lights and magnetic signs on the sides saying 'Exterminator', pulls up slowly at the end of Cherry Lane. The car comes to a stop six doors down from Mr. Parabolikos' house - the yucky mustard yellow one on the corner.

They exit the vehicle and Wingwing climbs into the trunk where he changes clothes. Schnitzkof protects him from view using his suit jacket spread wide like a flasher might.

A woman passing by, pushing a baby stroller, elicits a loud sound of disgust by what she interprets and rushes down the street away from the duo. Schnitzkof then closes his coat and WingWing emerges from the trunk wearing a boy scout uniform, which come to think of it, doesn't look all that different from his little police uniform.

The good General plunges his head into the truck, fiddles around for a moment then reappears wearing a priest's collar, owl-like eyeglasses and fake droopy ears.

"I sure hope he has my cream puff.", pouts WingWing, as our trusty investigators make their way down the street, using the trees for cover, so as not to be spotted by the creepy, nasty, tall, squirrelly Mr. Parabolikos. Right now, he's standing at the bottom of his porch looking through binoculars, away from the direction that Schnitzkof and WingWing are approaching.

A blue bird flies off from a nearby tree. Mr. Parabolikos appears to be following the bird's movement but he's actually zeroed in on a little boy who's walking to the schoolyard across the street.

The schoolyard is filled with children playing on outdoor gyms and swings. Mr. Parabolikos' watches, salivating, and a thick drool trickles down his chin. His knee is bouncing up and down like he's humping himself.

WingWing cuts through a side yard of the house as Schnitzkof walks nonchalantly up to the pervert. "Lots of weather we're having.", he announces pleasantly.

Mr. Parabolikos keeps looking through the binoculars. "Yeah, what of it?", he responds nastily. His knee action comes to a halt.

"Well, nothing, really, I was just trying to make conversation as any friendly neighbor might."

"Well, don't.", says the the nasty s.o.b.

"Oh, look", points the General, "there's a pretty little blue bird. Might I have a look through your binoculars?"

Mr. Parabolikos spins around, while still looking through his binoculars, and comes face to face with the owl-eyed Schnitzkof. All he sees are the General's eyes peering back at him.

Meanwhile, at Mr. Parabolikos' house, WingWing is squeezing his round little body through a doggy door and pops up inside the kitchen where, curled in his little bed with a leash around his neck and tied tightly to a pantry door, is a sad Bull Terrier. The poor pup barely lifts his head when he spots WingWing from the corner of his eye.

WingWing quickly rifles through the refrigerator looking for his cream puff and then moves onto the kitchen cabinets. The dog finally becomes interested as WingWing searches through the trash. He tries to play with WingWing but can't move much because of the tight leash. WingWing approaches the dog who perks up further and wags his tail.

Nearby are food and water dishes while the pup's squeaky toy is well out of reach. WingWing sniffs the food dish which has long been empty just like the water bowl. He then pries open the dog's mouth to smell his breath -- nothing. The poor little pup whimpers sadly.

WingWing turns to leave when he spots the dog's squeaky toy. He stares at the dog then the toy. And then, somehow touched by the dog's sadness, he moves the toy closer to him. The dog, straining at the leash, pushes the toy back at WingWing with his nose, trying to engage him in play.

WingWing checks the wall clock, then anxious by the time spent in the house, he quickly moves back toward the doggy door, which causes the dog to whimper louder.

Rattled, WingWing looks through the window and spots Mr. Parabolikos reacting to the noise and Schnitzkof pretending to have a coughing fit to cover for the commotion inside.

WingWing turns to the dog, then back to the door. He pauses for a moment then makes a mad dash for the doggy door and plows on through, causing the dog to simply drop sadly back onto his bed. A moment later, WingWing reemerges in the kitchen and the dog perks up.

WingWing quickly unties the leash from the pantry, grabs the dog up in his arms and pockets the squeaky toy. He pushes back through the doggy door, made all the more difficult with the pup in his arms, licking his face.

Outside the house, Mr. Parabolikos is still enjoying his view of the schoolyard as Schnitzkof spots WingWing with the dog hurrying away from the house. "Well", says the General, "I guess it's time for me to attend to my own flock. Good day to you, Sir."

Schnitzkof rushes off down the street and arrives at his police car where WingWing is waiting with the dog. "What on earth are you doing with that scraggly dog? Wait ... is that Mr. Parabolikos' dog?"

"Yes, Sir, that fiend has been abusing him. Look, General, he's hungry and thirsty."

Schnitzkof peers closely at the dog who looks so pathetic. "Is that true?"

"Oh for sure, oh General. It 's horrible."

"Well that really gets my goat!"

"I beg your pardon, Sir."

"My goat, WingWing. That gets my goat. Have you never heard that expression?"

WingWing places the dog on the back seat of the police car. "My grandfather had a goat."

"Yes, well, that's very nice that your grandfather had a goat but it just means I'm highly irked and agitated to say the least. Mad as hell, in fact. If there's one thing I really hate it's people who abuse animals. They should be shot on sight ... if not before."

WingWing climbs back into the trunk to change clothes. "Oh, yes, General, I agree wholeheartedly."

Schnitzkof deflates the giant ant and removes the exterminator signs from the car. As WingWing climbs out of the trunk, the General throws the disguises in, including what he's wearing.

"You make sure you move that animal abusing pig-fart pervert up on the list.", he orders.

"I will, Sir ... So can I keep him? Huh? Can I? Can I?"

They hop into the car and adjust their seat belts. Schnitzkof checks his mirrors, catching sight of the dog in the back seat. The pup's doing one of those looney circling routines before lying down and making himself comfortable.

"I guess so ... If we had caught that pinprick of a bird-watching Peeping Tom in action last month ... then he might not have been around to have abused that poor dog."

The dog's ears perk up and Schnitzkof drives off with a jolt causing WingWing to grab hold of the dashboard to steady himself.

The clock reads noon. Lunchtime. Police Car 54 parks outside Avalon Super-Duper Market & Sundries.

WingWing runs into the store and returns a few minutes later carrying a grocery bag. "Look, General, I got him some food." WingWing hops in and quickly pops open a can of dog food. He reaches over the back seat and serves it to pup in a sparkling new bowl.

The dog eats eagerly as WingWing breaks out a sandwich, which he shares with Schnitzkof, along with a cup of coffee and a short bottle of milk.

They munch away while watching the various passersby including a mime who's pretending to be a clown stuffing himself into an imaginary car.

"So, General, are our leads getting cold?"

"Fear not, little chum, I'm certain there will be a break in the case very soon. Now ... who's next on the list?"

WingWing juggles his sandwich as he pulls out his note pad. "Let's see. It looks like Juniper Wiggins. Sir, do we really need to keep Mrs. Wiggins on the list? She only killed once and almost got off for it."

"Once a killer always a killer."

"But is a killer always a thief?" asks the ever curious WingWing.

"Well, let's see ... How much wood would a woodchuck chuck ... if a woodchuck could chuck wood?"

WingWing blinks in confusion.

Schnitzkof continues, "He would chuck, he would, as much as he could. And chuck as much as

Buddy
After a Good Meal and Lots of Love

a woodchuck would if a woodchuck could chuck wood."

Still nothing from WingWing.

"E equals M C squared?", queries the General, then ... after a pause ... "Good lord, WingWing, does nothing register with you?"

"So does that mean that a killer is always a thief?

Exasperated, the General replies with a simple "Yes".

"Wow! That's amazing. I wish I could figure things out like that."

"You will. It's in the cards, my boy. Maybe not as soon as I had hoped, but someday."

Schnitzkof drives off en route to Mrs. Wiggins' house.

WingWing looks back at the dog, who's now resting comfortably. "I've decided to name him Buddy."

The pup raises and tilts his head in approval.

"You like that ... huh ... Buddy?"

"BARK BARK." Of course he does! It's the first real name he's ever had.

"That's a fine name for a dog, WingWing. Did I ever tell you about the dog I had when I was a young whippersnapper?"

"No, Sir, was he as cute as Buddy?"

Schnitzkof peers at his rear view mirror at Buddy. "Well, I'll let you be the judge. I keep his picture in the glove box there. Have a look."

WingWing searches through the paper and candy filled glove box and finds a photo of "Butch", Schnitzkof's killer German Shepherd with teeth bared and frothy slobber all over this face.

"You said he was your pet when you were a child?"

"Yes."

WingWing looks long and hard at Schnitzkof as if he's thinking 'WTF' just as Police Car 54 arrives at 100 Peppermill Lane - Mrs. Wiggins House - a spotless little number with a large yard sign that reads: 'Killer Lives Here'.

Schnitzkof and WingWing exit the car while Buddy sits up and watches as our detectives march up the front porch steps.

Old Lady Wiggins is in a rocker knitting.

"Good day to you, Mrs. Wiggins.", says the General, "I see you're looking healthy and spry these days."

Mrs. Wiggins actually looks like a load of dried crap wrapped in a tattered bathrobe. She smiles sweetly at Schnitzkof.

Then out blurts WingWing, "Did you take my cream puff?"

Mrs. Wiggins' smile rapidly dissipates.

"Ah, what Officer WingWing is trying to say ... or ask, rather ... is ... where were you roughly four hours ago when his cream puff went missing in the French Quarter?"

"Four hours ago, you say? Four hours ... let me see. I'm sitting here knitting as you can well see. I've completed ..." *the old woman quickly counts her knitting rows,* "... twelve rows. Two rows an hour.

That makes six hours sitting here knitting. Leaving two hours more than your four hour window. Which means I did not steal Officer WingWing's or any other person's cream puff. As for the French Quarter which resides approximately 3 miles to the west and with no bus stop even though it's a big tourist attraction and big money maker for this town ... you very well know I don't own a car nor even a telephone to call a taxi ... and my neighbors are all at work so they can't give me a lift ... and besides, as you well know" ... *now flashing her ankle monitor* ... "I am not even allowed off my porch. So, how the heck do you think I could get to the French Quarter anyway? Now, it seems to me, unless you received a 'not-so-violent-criminal-on-the-loose-alert', I am wondering why you would drive all this way across town to question me about a cream puff that I could not possibly have stolen now or ever. Nor could I even have eaten such a delectable dessert, being a long-diagnosed type-two diabetic, as you well know. This is yet another case of police harassment and I'm going to make a note of it and write a letter to the County Attorney to take action against you and your whole department. And, as you well know, once I do that, you will be put on suspension with no back pay and you'll be fined a month's salary at the very least. As for you and your little companion, you should very well know that a false accusation will get the Society Against False Accusations on your dumb asses and they will picket your offices and your homes until you've reconciled the damages you've caused."

Whew!

It's a stare down. Schnitzkof then whips out his wallet and offers her a twenty dollar bill. She scowls. He slips out another. No dice. And another. She snatches the damn thing from his hand and empties the contents into her own then silently offers back the wallet. And with that, our detectives remove themselves from Old Lady Wiggins' front porch.

"Better take her name off the list.", says an exasperated Schnitzkof.

Our trusty duo moves along and takes a break at the little dog park a few streets away. WingWing fills a bowl from the water fountain and serves some delicious, cool wet water to Buddy.

"Perhaps we're going about this the wrong way.", admits the General, "Maybe we need to start at the beginning."

"But General, we still have two more of the usual suspects. Well ... three more if you count the Maloney Brothers as two instead of one."

Schnitzkof's shoulders shake in fright at the mere mention of their names again.

There are loud sniffs from Buddy who's sniffing around their feet and as far as he can go on the leash.

"What to do? What to do? If only we had some way of tracking the cream puff." ponders Schnitzkof.

More frantic sniffing from Buddy. Schnitzkof looks at him. "Now what on earth is he going on about? Did you step in some doo-doo or something?", he asks WingWing.

WingWing checks his shoes, "No, my General."

They both watch Buddy sniff around the base of the water fountain.

"Maybe Buddy can help.", says WingWing.

Buddy starts digging.

"Nonsense. It takes months or even years of rigorous training to turn a dog into a tracker. Buddy's been living in a psycho peeper's house all this time. What does he know of the odors of the world around him?"

Buddy digs up a hamster carcass. He drops it proudly at the General's feet. Schnitzkof and WingWing exchange looks.

"Back to the French Quarter!", Schnitzkof orders.

Police Car 54 arrives screeching back at the French Quarter. Lovely French Café music plays as before. And Schnitzkof and WingWing, with Buddy in tow, barrel out of the car.

Outside Monet's French Café, Chef Monet is bussing an outdoor table. He becomes distracted by tapping sounds. Schnitzkof and WingWing stroll in arm and arm, wearing dark sunglasses and fake noses combos and berets while the General is pretending to use a white cane for the blind. Buddy, on a leash, leads the way, sniffing frantically. The Chef continues working but seems suspicious.

Slyly and loudly, the General proclaims "Oh ... from the smell of it, I think we must have reached that fabulous patisserie shop everyone has told us about."

Buddy sniffs around the table where the duo were sitting earlier. He goes back to WingWing and sniffs his shoe. Buddy then takes off trotting and sniffing, heading in the opposite direction from the front entrance to the French Quarter.

"It's a good thing we have this diabetes prevention dog with us.", Schnitzkof continues loudly while tapping his cane wildly from side to side in an effort to keep up with WingWing and Buddy. He accidentally whacks an old lady in the ass.

"Owww!"

Turning his head to apologize, "I beg your pardon, Madame." When the General turns back face forward, he crashes into an old man.

"Watch where you're going!" shouts the annoyed old timer.

"Sir. Excuse me. My cane doesn't appear to be working very well today."

When they're all far enough from Chef Monet's they stop and remove their disguises, shoving them into their various pockets.

"My word, WingWing. You know I can't run that fast."

Buddy's straining at the leash.

"Sorry, my General, but Buddy's really picked up the scent. We need to hurry up and follow him."

Schnitzkof bends down to Buddy, more in an effort to catch his breath. "Good dog, good dog. So you have the scent, do you?" Buddy licks Schnitzkof's face wildly. "Then off with you ... little helpful hound."

And they're off, out the back end of the French Quarter.

Buddy's nose is to the ground, sniffing, sniffing and more sniffing. They pass people, trees, buildings, parks, more people and on and on it goes as they traverse the town in search of WingWing's missing cream puff.

Eventually they land in a seedy part of town. Sadly, every town has one, even Avalon. Schnitzkof, WingWing and Buddy turn a corner.

"I'm getting awfully tired, oh General."

"Yes, it has been a rather exhausting day."

They spot three homeless people warming themselves over a trash can fire. And just then, from around another corner, a fourth homeless man approaches, pushing a shopping cart that's filled to the brim with junk which also happen to be everything in this world the man owns. After greeting his friends, he produces from under a shabby blanket, a paper plate with WingWing's cream puff on it! The other men delight in the scrumptious gift.

WingWing's eyes widen too, "But ... that's my ..."

"Easy, little chum.", Schnitzkof grips WingWing's shoulder.

"But ... but ..."

The cream puff carrying man produces a plastic knife from his dirty pocket and carefully cuts the delectable dessert into four evenly proportioned slices, offering each to a friend and taking the remaining one for himself.

Schnitzkof and WingWing look at each other, now saddened and yet humbled by the spectacle. Buddy whimpers. They watch again as the group savors every last morsel of their prizes.

Buddy reacts as a ratty dog runs over to the homeless men. The bearer of the gift puts the paper plate down so the dog can lick it. His tail wags happily. Buddy's too, in empathy.

Schnitzkof and WingWing silently do an about face and walk away, hands clasped in friendship, and encouraged by the fact that they have solved their case.

Buddy, who's walking next to WingWing, bumps his nose up to WingWing's hand for a good petting.

It's been a long day, indeed. Birds flap their tired wings past the threesome on their way to a tall tree for a restful night's sleep and General Schnitzkof, his trusted companion WingWing and helpful hound Buddy literally walk off into the sunset.

Yes, sometimes happiness is as simple as a warm cream puff and a cold wet nose.

CASE CLOSED.

<u>Note to Editor:</u> Times Tribune Post, Upper America:

Mr. Parabolikos has replica of school yard in his living room. STOP

Madame Judge plays with herself at the brothel. STOP

Next case file: I'll let you know. STOP

Till next time. This is Ginger Marin reporting from Avalon, over and out.

About the Author

Ginger Marin is a former network TV Journalist at NBC News NY, where she served as producer and writer for the network's "News-on-the-Hour"; "Sunday Today", "Nightly News-Weekend Edition", "NBC News Overnight" and various news specials. Ginger has written for Tom Brokaw, Maria Shriver, Roger Mudd, Linda Ellerbee, Garrick Utley and numerous other news anchors. She was a news feed producer and news writer for NBC's Affiliate News Service, servicing the network's 200 affiliates and also worked for Visnews, a London-based international news agency. Ginger is currently a freelance writer and actor living in Los Angeles, CA. To learn more about Ginger's acting projects, visit http://www.imdb.me/gingermarin

Connect With Ginger

Website: GingerMarin.com

Twitter: @Ginger_Marin

Blog: BionicLady.com

Facebook Profile: http://www.facebook.com/gingermarin.actor

Facebook Page: http://www.facebook.com/AdventuresInAvalon

Happy Trails From Ginger

Writing Adventures in Avalon was a rewarding experience for me and I certainly hope you feel the same after having read it. If you enjoyed the adventure and would like to post a review, please do so on the book's page at Amazon. Your review would be invaluable to me. Also, feel free to reach out to me at any one of my above connection points. It would be great to hear from you.

Thank you and best regards,

Ginger

Printed in Great
Britain
by Amazon